THE SINS OF SEVEN SERIES

ENVY

DANI RENÉ

Published by Dani René

Second Edition Paperback ISBN: 978-1-8384492-4-7

eBook ISBN: 978-0-639-95736-4

The following story contains mature themes, strong language, and sexual situations. It is intended for adult readers.

This book is a work of fiction. Names, characters, places, and incidents either are products of the author's imagination or are used fictitiously. Any resemblance to actual events or locales or persons, living or dead, is entirely coincidental.

WARNING

In a world of secrets, where sins are hidden from sight, people live their lives hoping that those around them never know what desires they conceal. The darkest needs, those that taunt just below the surface. Those they hide in the deepest recesses of their minds. Those things they don't admit to. The things they don't talk about. That's what this series touches on. You may find some of the subject matter disturbing, you may even look away, cringe, and gasp. But that's why I wanted to write these seven couples. These couples came to me with their confessions and I obeyed their need to have their stories told. The dark, depraved, the taboo. The things we may find tempting, alluring, and may even be turned on by it. That's what I wanted to write.

Each story is an interconnected standalone, delving into the relationship of the couples you'll meet. There will be sex, there will most certainly be foul language. And there will DEFINITELY be taboo subjects covered.

The Sins of Seven revolves around seven couples who are so different in nature, in what their likes and dislikes are. They're each unique in desire, in their personalities, and even in the way they try to show affection. They don't love. At least, they don't think they do, they don't believe they're worthy of it.

Each story will make a point of focusing on one of the seven deadly sins.

Greed, Pride, Lust, Gluttony, Sloth, Wrath, Envy.

Although they'll be released in their own order, you'll be able to tell which sin, follows which couple and their journey to possibly find their happily ever after.

Please heed this warning.

**This is a dark romance, suitable for mature audiences, 18+ ONLY. Strong sexual themes and violence, which could trigger emotional distress, are found in this story. Certain scenes are graphic and could be upsetting to some. This story is NOT for everyone. Proceed with caution. Discretion is advised.*

Dedication

To the readers who've supported me through this journey. I love you, your encouragement and kind words mean the world to me.

Dani xo

Playlist

- Desire - Meg Myers
- Black Widow - Iggy Azalea, Rita Ora
- The After You - Miakoda
- Unsteady - X Ambassadors
- Low Life - Future, The Weeknd
- In the Night - The Weeknd
- Love Faces - Tre Songz
- Silhouette - Birdy
- Monster - Meg Myers
- My way - Tom Walker
- Walk Through The Fire - Mary Gauthier

Find the full playlist on Spotify

"Love does not envy."

Unknown

Prologue

Six years ago

The rain trickling from the sky offers a light dusting of silvery jewels that settles on the black coats and umbrellas surrounding the grave. I can't drag my eyes away from the grass, shimmering with each of the glassy drops. Colors contrast around each other. Black from the mourners and green blades of grass beneath our feet, along with the murky gray of the sky and the dark brown of the earth that will soon cover the coffin. Bright red roses sit in a vase awaiting their final resting place atop the wood and metal casket.

The sounds of sniffling from the mourners and soft prayers from the priest echo through the fog. I reflect on the last moment I saw my father alive and I'm reminded of him smiling at me, telling me he loved me.

My eyes travel over each person, taking them in. Every face in the crowd is one I've seen at the house since I was old enough to be allowed into the living room when we had visitors. I recall the instances I met them. Family dinners. Charity functions. Even my junior and high school graduations. They're all here to say goodbye to the man they no longer serve. A man who no longer pays their salaries or furnishes them with gifts so expensive they'll never have to work again if they sold those priceless offerings.

But none of them know who he truly was. They didn't see the ruthless man I grew up with. He taught me everything about being vigilant with strangers. People didn't like him; they feared him, and that's why they're here today. Some to say goodbye, others to be thankful he spared their lives. I don't blame them for the anger they feel. What hurts the most is now I'm alone. The Calloway name that was worn proudly by my sister and me will soon be forgotten. When my sister died at the tender age of sixteen, Daddy made sure I didn't feel alone by spending as much time with me as he could. He showed me how the organization worked, what he

influenced, and who he ruled over.

When I think about Meredith, I recall her like she's standing beside me. But she's no longer here. Closing my eyes, I picture her, imagining how she'd be dressed for our father's funeral. Her dress would be the color of a raven's feathers with her hair matching the sleek silky material. Dark lines would be penciled in beneath her silver eyes. They're beautiful, yet unnaturally gray, so much so that they appear the same color as the metal of the coffin. Even though we're twins, I'm the complete opposite.

My white hair hangs down my back in waves the color of snow. The green in my eyes is almost luminous. Perhaps even matching the freshly cut grass we're standing on. When I'm angry, it darkens to the color of the oak trees behind the Calloway mansion.

"Help the young lady as she grieves, Father. In the midst of the sadness, ensure her belief and trust in the communion of saints, the forgiveness of earthly sins, and the resurrection to the life everlasting. Amen," Pastor Micheli murmurs as he throws a handful of the dirt onto my father's lowering coffin into his final resting place.

Somehow, I doubt God would even look my way. The sins of Victor Ernest Calloway are too dark and far too violent for him to ever find forgiveness. I know this because I've seen what he can do, what he has done.

People start moving slowly, each one taking a rose from the vase, releasing it into the hole my father will now lie in forever. I don't cry. Tears don't even threaten my eyes as I watch each scarlet bud fall.

All I see is darkness.

Revenge.

Black.

I no longer allow any other emotion into my chest, into my life. Once the mourners have finished, I step forward alone. An ache in my chest appears so acute it steals my breath. I'm no longer part of a family. At least, not one I remembered as a child.

Seventeen years old and an orphan.

My eyes don't blink as I take a handful of dirt and allow it to hit the wood with a thud. The hand that settles on my shoulder reminds me of what I have to do. When I turn to him, he offers me a gentle smile. As violent as he is handsome, the man I've known almost

all my life is here for me. A touch that seems to tell me *don't worry, you'll be okay*. Hazel eyes pierce me; they look right through me. Like they always have.

No words are spoken as he leads me away. My head is bowed, allowing my long hair to fall like a curtain around my face. I don't want people to sympathize with me. I don't need their words of commiseration. My heart has hardened. Rock solid in its cage.

One day soon, I'll be drenched in the blood of the man who stole my family from me. And when I am, I want to see the life drain from his eyes. And there's only one way I'll be able to do that. I need to become stronger, colder, more malevolent than my father was.

I have to walk through the dark to find the light.

ELIANA

Present Day

I was twelve when my father first told me I'd one day work for him. He told me I was special. When I was seventeen, I watched his coffin get lowered into the ground, six feet under. He was murdered brutally in his own home.

I was sent to live with one of my father's best friends. A man I'd grown up calling uncle. Sean Briggs could never replace Dad, but he gave me the love and nurturing I needed. He was tall with broad shoulders, a full head of salt and pepper hair, and dark scruff that hid his jawline. His eyes were brown, so dark they were almost onyx. A kind smile that I'm sure had hidden horrors behind it. I knew he had his own organization, dealing in weapons and drugs, but so did my father.

Both men were feared when they walked into a room dressed in their immaculate suits. They also never got their hands dirty. That's why I started training the moment I stepped foot on the Briggs compound.

I completed my first *job* six months later. Sean walked in and smiled. Found me with blood all over my clothes, hands, and face. I was young, the youngest he'd ever trained besides his two sons. When he complimented me on the shots, I was filled with elation at the pride in his eyes, but there was nothing that could prepare me for the bloodlust that seemed to grow within me.

He told me I would soon be ready. That I could go out in the field with the rest of the men, and I'd be able to work undercover. Because of my looks, I could take down a man easily by luring him to his destruction.

My first kill, I had Sean watch me like a hawk. Even though the man I'd shot was a criminal, I hesitated for a moment before Sean gave me the encouragement I needed to make the kill. He whispered in my ear that I should imagine this was my father's killer, and that's what I did. My finger pressed the trigger quickly. But it was my second kill with Michael, O'Connoll—the man

who trained me—that changed me. I don't know why I enjoyed what I did, but I reveled in it.

Many times over the past four years, I realized any normal person would have been fearful of that. I wasn't. And since then, I haven't looked back because each time I take a shot, I recall Michael's words in my mind. I want to be ready for the day I get to find the man who murdered my father and when that day comes, I'll ensure nothing stops me from taking his life.

It's been years since I returned home, even after being held captive for those few months by a man I thought I loved, I didn't come to the place I grew up in. Instead, I found family in Chicago with Peyton and Carrick, as well as Mason and Savannah.

But now that I'm here, I find nothing has changed. The moment I stepped foot back in Riverfield, I knew I couldn't leave until I unearthed the secrets that have been locked in my mind since I was sixteen.

I should go home, to the house I grew up in, but my mind isn't ready for the onslaught just yet. I know I'm broken. I know that no matter how hard I try to live a normal life, I can't. The only place I have solace now is

with Sean. He's given me a home, and I've accepted.

Stalking toward the Briggs mansion, I notice a black Jeep sitting at the entrance to the driveway. The house sits on acres of land, with gardens that would give the Royals a run for their money. The cobblestone weaves itself from the ornate metal gates at the entrance to the house a few hundred yards away.

I push open the enormous dark oak door and step inside. The house is quiet as I make my way toward the staircase. It's when I reach the second floor that I hear music blaring from one of the rooms. Since I've been here, I haven't met either of the Briggs boys. I'm curious if one of them has come home.

Being back in the Briggs mansion, I recall the time I spent here after my father died, and all that time, I don't remember either son visiting.

The harsh sound of heavy metal screams at me even though the door is closed. The walls, dark and somber, vibrate to the guitar riffs and heavy drums. I smile and head up to the third floor where my attic bedroom awaits me.

Stepping into my bedroom, I turn on the iPod and

flop onto the bed. Music has always been my escape. I would get lost in a melody, in the rhythm. It's the only way I could focus my anger besides fighting. That . . . and sex. I lost my virginity when I was seventeen to Michael who'd been training me to fight, to kill, and to ultimately get revenge on my father's killer. He was my first, but he is most definitely not my last. He showed me how to murder without leaving evidence, but did more than teach me those skills. I became addicted to how hard he'd take me. Anywhere and everywhere. We'd satiate the hunger with fucking and killing. Quickly, I learned how to find pleasure while appeasing my rage.

Shaking my head of the violent yet sexual thoughts, I close my eyes and picture the scene that has haunted me for years. The coffin. The crying. The pain on everyone's faces.

Picking up my phone, I hit dial on the number that's been my saving grace every time I've felt the need to go off the rails. Each time I have an urge to do something stupid, he's been there for me.

The ringing on the other end matches each beat of my thudding heart. Memories of what he taught me,

how he trained me, and the promise he made plays in my mind.

Michael O'Connell is the only man who can get me up to par for the moment I've been working towards. He's the one man I know I can trust. He's been investigating the murder, and I hope soon we'll have results. I want a name. It's been far too long already.

"Eliana," he murmurs my name.

"Michael, how are you?" I ask. Pushing off the bed, I stroll over to the window. I know he can't see me, but something about his deep breaths calms me. I am still dressed in my black, knee-length skirt with my stockings sitting at my thighs and the garter that holds them up hugging my hips.

"I'm well. Is there anything I can do for you, sweetheart?" he asks, but I can read into the tone of his voice. He's not offering me help with the investigation; he's asking if I need a fuck. We've tried to keep our relationship a secret because if Sean ever found out I was sleeping with Michael, he'd lose his shit.

When I first met Michael, I was much younger. Fleeting memories of him invade my mind at times, but

for the most part, I don't recall much from my teenage years. Michael towers over me at almost six-two. He is built like a bodyguard, wide shoulders with tightly packed muscle. The dark, messy hair that hangs into his hazel eyes always looks like it's windblown. His face reminds me of a painting — perfect, smooth with a prominent jaw, and sharp nose.

He's handsome. Breathtakingly so. On the outside, he looks like he should be on the runway for Gucci or Versace. But it's on the inside that the man himself turns into a beast. Michael is one of the best killers on the team. His methods are clean, unsuspecting, and he's worked for this family for far too long.

When I left, he didn't want to speak to me. He was angry I chose someone else over him, but the young heart wanted what it wanted. And I ran off into the sunset and found out it was the biggest mistake of my life.

Granted, he is twelve years older than me, but age is merely a number. At least, that's what I believe. Other people in this house would probably not feel the same way. So, we've kept our trysts to the basement where we train, his car, or his apartment, which is a small log cabin

on the Briggs compound.

"Michael, don't start that right now. I can't see you till tomorrow. But I do need your help."

"Anything for you, Eliana," he responds confidently. Everything Michael does is done with passion, ferocity, and focus. He's a predator in every sense of the word, and when he has a mark, there's no stopping him.

"I need to know who killed, Dad. We need to take them down. I'm going to ask Sean to find the name. He has connections." My words cause him to inhale sharply.

"Eliana, I know you're angry—"

"This isn't anger, Michael. It's vengeance." My words are poison, and I will ensure they seep into the veins of the asshole when we find him. I want to bathe in his filthy blood and revel in his demise. He took my family from me, and I'm done playing games.

"I understand that, but I'll warn you, once you walk farther into this world, you may never come out. Mr. Briggs runs some dark organizations, sweetheart. What you've seen is only the tip of the iceberg. You need to understand that."

"I'm not afraid of playing in the dark. If you can't

help me, I'll find someone who can," I retort. Frustration ebbs and flows through me. I thought he'd be the one to be there for me. I figured he'd understand.

"If you want to walk into their sordid world, I'll do my best to prepare you. We'll train in the morning. Don't forget . . . Once you kill for revenge, it will change you forever." His warning squeezes the breath from my lungs. I know this won't be easy. But I have to do something.

"I don't have another choice, Michael. You know that," I tell him, feeling my confidence slip.

He sighs in response, and I know he's disappointed that I've chosen to go to Sean. Even though he's worked for the man for so long, he knows how dark this world is.

"I'll be there for you, Eliana. Every step of the way." His promise hovers in the air around me, keeping me warm in its embrace. Every time this man talks to me, I feel safe. As if he's the only person who will be there for me. "I just want you to be careful."

"I will, Michael. I will."

He hangs up without a goodbye, which squeezes

my heart. Even though he confirmed he's behind me, supporting me, there's a niggling feeling deep in my gut that something is going to go wrong. Like the world is about to crash in on me and I'm going to be left stranded on the shore.

"Can you do this, Eliana?" Michael's voice comes from behind me. I know I can. The gun in my hand is cool, heavy, and loaded, ready to take out the asshole who's in the car in front of us. He doesn't know we're here, but we know where he's headed.

"I've been training for six months. I've never been more ready, Michael," I tell him earnestly because I feel it down to my core. I was born for this. And finishing this job for Sean will only show him how much I appreciate his help. His guidance. And it will also be the first step into getting stronger. I need to if I'm going to kill the man who murdered my father.

The pier is up ahead, and our mark turns into the parking lot only meters from where we're stopped. I watch him exit his vehicle, a small gun in his hand. He's dressed in black. We watch as he makes his way

into the empty warehouse. We played him, and we did it well. Michael and I exit the SUV and head into the back entrance of the large building.

"Who are you, little girl?" the asshole sneers when he sees me. They always underestimate the girl. I'm fragile looking, but I'm definitely not a toy that can be broken. "You come to play with the big boys?" He chuckles as I near him. That's when Michael steps out from the shadows.

"I wouldn't make her angry," he tells our mark. The man I'm about to murder.

"Why? Is she going to throw a tantrum?" I watch him laugh. I smile as he shakes his head in disbelief, then I raise my hand. The silver glint of the 9mm in my grip shimmers in the dim light and those dark eyes that once held amusement now flicker with curiosity. "You shouldn't play with adult toys, little girl."

"Fuck you," I hiss, pulling the trigger. The bullet makes contact with his arm, and I watch his gun fall from his hand. The clatter echoes around us, and he grunts in agony.

"You little bitch!"

"Yes, I am." I step closer, my body spinning and twisting

with my leg straight out. My foot makes contact with his face, and the roundhouse kick I've been practicing looks incredible from my view as I hear the crack of his jawbone. Blood spurts from his mouth. His teeth drenched in the crimson liquid. "Don't ever underestimate a girl," I tell him on a shrug, pulling the trigger again, ensuring the bullet meets his chest. I watch in awe as his body falls to the ground, his eyes wide with shock, and I shrug again. "Nice knowing you, asshole."

"Not bad, baby girl. Not bad at all." Michael's voice comes from behind me. His body Is pressing against my ass. "You look hot killing him," he whispers along my neck. His lips feather on the sensitive skin, causing me to tremble with need. The exhilaration of the kill is still burning through my veins. The grip he has on my hips causes me to whimper. I'm turned on by my first real kill.

"Fuck me, Michael. Take me home and fuck me."

And he does, until I pass out.

The memory makes me smile. The training we did today hurt like a bitch. My body aches in places I didn't know I had muscles. Even though I've done a similar style of fighting before, this was brutal. The looming

building of my college is in front of me as I make my way toward the entrance. Gray skies and the sprinkling of rain does nothing to improve my mood.

I'm about to walk through the doors when I feel someone watching me. An electric current seems to crackle in the air, warning me not to turn around. I step forward, but as I do, another jolt of lightning cracks wildly, shooting through me.

I turn to find a stranger standing in the quad. He's dressed all in black. The leather jacket shimmers with raindrops. His dark hair matches the raven color of his jeans that seem to hug his muscled thighs. Heavy black boots that adorn his feet remind me of the ones Michael wears.

I haven't seen him on campus before, and my interest is piqued. The moment his deep-brown eyes meet mine, my heart thuds in my chest wildly. He's every bit the heartthrob I have a penchant for — dark, brooding, dangerous. His gaze trails over me from head to toe, which causes my stomach to flip flop and my breathing to hitch.

It feels as if we're the only two people in the world

and I'm tethered to him. I can't explain it. Not even Michael has made my body react so intensely. The corner of this stranger's mouth lifts into a smirk that ignites a yearning deep in my gut. Even though there's a danger emanating from him, something tells me he could be more lethal to my body than my life.

He finally moves, breaking the spell. His steps are slow but methodical as he nears me. Each female who passes by him can't help look. Almost every girl smiles at him, but his gaze is pinned on me, rooting me to the spot. He's not fazed by any of them. At first, curiosity swirls in my chest when I see another pretty blonde, stunning brunette, or sultry raven-haired girl sidle up to him, but his eyes are trained on his mark, focusing on one girl.

Me.

I must admit, he is handsome beyond measure. The smooth, tanned skin of his chiseled jaw ticks when he reaches me. He stops inches from where I'm standing, but I can't bring myself to step back, or even breathe.

"Eliana Calloway." My name on his lips, on his tongue, sends a sliver of desire through me. I glance up

and come face to face with one of the most handsome men I've ever seen. A dangerous, alluring, and intriguing man I know is about to pull me deep into a dark abyss.

How do I know?

It's easy.

The way his eyes rove over my body, the small quirk of the corner of his mouth which makes the dimples in his cheeks even more prominent, and the aura of darkness that seems to cloud around him. Tell-tale signs. All that I ignore when I smile and step even closer to him.

"Depends who's asking," I utter with an attempt to keep my voice level.

He shrugs, not offering a response. His dark gaze takes me in, every single inch of me as he steps around me. From the Converse on my feet to the top of my windblown white locks of hair.

"It's my job to make sure I know everything there is to know about the most talked about girl in town," he says. His voice is rich, thick, and raspy, but decadent, like a creamy hot chocolate that warms you on a cold winter's night. And with November around the corner, the chill of the wind has nothing on this man.

"You shouldn't believe everything you hear. What are you doing here, Asher?" I risk a curious glance at him. I keep my stance shoulder-width apart and my hands at my sides.

He notices this, from the small shift in my posture to the way my fingers grip the textbook in my hand. His mouth quirks, the corner lifting slightly, and his dimples appear again. "Figured I'd follow you home," he says. He's aloof, but like a hunter, he watches my every move. "I arrived a few days ago, and I wanted to see what was more important than learning to kneel for me at Seven Sins."

His head tips to the side, causing his messy black hair to fall into his hypnotic brown eyes, and his dark brows furrow.

"Tell me something, Eliana. When did you last taste the rush of danger? Feel the thick, warm liquid, the sweet crimson life force of another drip from your fingertips? Did it get you wet?"

The words, the question, everything sends my mind reeling, and I feel lightheaded. A cocktail of anxiety, fear, and wariness overcomes me. In my attempt to step back

from him, I stumble, the ground nearing me, but I don't make an impact because his hands are around my waist. He pulls me to standing, then steps back, giving me room to breathe.

"Remember..." he says, his voice dropping low as it tickles my ear. "I know everything there is to know about you." He steps by me then, the movement slow but calculated. I know he's doing it to make sure I heard him. And I have. I've heard more than I'd like to. "See you around." Three words and he's gone.

My breathing is ragged. I'm affected by him. Fear and desire are a lethal combination, and they swirl around me like his aura. He knows about me. He knows who I am, but how can he? We only met in Chicago when I was taken in by Mason and Carrick. I have no idea what Asher wants from me, but I'll certainly find out.

I breathe deeply, attempting to calm my racing heart and jittery nerves. Making my way into the building, I try to focus on the meeting I have coming up with the dean. Getting a job is something I've wanted to do since I came home. Wishing a normal life and having it are

two very different things. I don't need to work, but it's the only thing I can have that will allow me to focus on something other than killing the man who murdered my father.

As soon as Dean Latham enters the office, he smiles in greeting. "Miss Calloway, let's talk."

The moment I step out of the building, knowing I might have a job in the next few weeks, I take a deep calming breath. But I feel his white-hot gaze burning a hole through me. Mr. Tall, Dangerous, and Handsome stalks closer to me, and I wonder just what he's doing here.

"You're back."

"Stuck around; wanted to see you again," he smirks. Leaning in, his lips brush against the shell of my ear, and his warm breath — minty and fresh — wafts over me. "Let's play a game, Eliana," he says quietly as to not bring attention to us from any of the students meandering around the quad.

"And what game is that?" My whispered question is directed over his shoulder. I can't bring myself to look

into his dark eyes. They're too penetrating; they see all of me. Those sordid corners of my mind I keep hidden, he knows they're there, and it makes me wary.

"Truth or dare."

ASHER

She doesn't respond. Her body shakes with hunger, longing. I feel it wafting from her like the sweet-scented perfume she's wearing that reminds me of lavender and vanilla.

"Truth or dare?" she questions, watching random students walk by. They don't even notice us. We could be any other couple talking about stupid shit — parties, a date, even exams, but we're not. "I don't normally play games, but since you're so insistent, I'll offer one of my truths for one of yours." Her voice is filled with confidence, but there's a hint of curiosity, which I've been banking on.

"Deal," I offer, leaning closer to her, inhaling her lavender and vanilla scent. "But I can't confirm you'd like any of my answers."

At thirty-five, I've been there and done that, as they

say. I'm only here, on this campus for one thing — the beauty standing in front of me.

"Are you going to tell me why you're really here?" she questions again, still not meeting my hungry gaze.

"I'm here to see that you remember what happened to you," I tell her confidently. When I asked for Oliver's help with what I'm about to do, he offered it readily. He explained he has a contact who can certainly assist and I'm banking on it because Ellie needs to remember.

I've known her for so long it feels like I'm coming home. Seeing her grown up into a beautiful yet dangerous woman, I feel cheated to have missed the years without her. When I was forced to leave, all I could do was walk away without even saying goodbye. She doesn't remember me or anything that happened.

As many times, as I've told myself it's better that way, I can't deny it anymore. I want her to remember. It's time for her to finally see the truth that we've been hiding all this time. She has to recall the night our lives changed drastically.

Eliana Calloway is the epitome of an angel. A dark one. Her hair is like silk that my fingers itch to grip in a

fist while I have her bent over my desk. With eyes the color of new leaves on a reborn tree in the spring, she looks innocent, but I know how devious the little vixen can be.

It's been years since I first saw her playing in the garden of her father's estate with her sister. I've seen her change from an awkward little girl to a stunning young woman filled with rage, like a butterfly that's just awakened from her cocoon. Even then, I knew she'd grow up to be the perfect little assassin, until I was forced to leave. I was fascinated with her the moment I laid eyes on her.

When she turned seventeen and buried her last remaining family member, I wanted to swoop in and steal her away. To keep her just for me, but I knew I couldn't. I stayed in Chicago, hoping to move on from her. Even Nate told me there's no way to walk away from *the one.*

I want nothing more than to delve into her mind. Being close to her, I was not prepared for the magnetism that sizzled between us when she first saw me in Sins, but she didn't recognize me, and I knew she wouldn't.

Each year that passed was torturous, waiting for the right time. And now that Eliana's back in the place it all changed, I have to make sure I get her to Oliver's contact in London who said he could help.

She doesn't know how well I actually know her, how deeply rooted my knowledge of her goes. Now that I've finally got her in my grasp, I don't want to let her go. Shaking my head, I glance around the space.

"I think you need to find another project to work on because I'm definitely not it. You know nothing about me."

Her confidence is like a drug. She's beautiful, strong, and lethal. Every time I've seen her take someone down, it made me hard as fucking steel. The video's dad showed me of her sessions with the trainer revealed this shy temptress, transforming to a raging killer. Her bloodlust is incredible. But that was before she was locked in a fucking dungeon by someone who called himself a Master. He was a monster, but he's gone now.

"Give me a chance, Ellie," I coo in her ear. "I know you want it. Deny me right now, and I'll leave." My lips feather over her cheek, and she whimpers. It's a slight

sound, but I hear it. "You won't regret it, I promise." Smiling, I turn and leave her at the car and head to my jeep with thoughts of getting my girl back.

Seeing her drenched in blood made me want to rip her clothes off and fuck her in the sickly metallic-scented liquid. My cock twitches at the thought, now wondering how her flavor would fill my senses mixed with the blood of our enemy. Only, she doesn't yet know we share the same adversary.

I want to be inside the beautiful little creature as I ask her to end the life of the one man who took everything from us. The vile monster who didn't cast a second glance when he walked away from the dead body on the ground oozing blood into the plush carpet.

The reason I came back is to make sure she remembers everything that happened to her. To us. She needs to recall the real reason she's lost everything, and only then can we all move forward. The secret we've all kept is long overdue in being revealed. And I am going to bring it to light.

Soon, I will have all the control, and she's going to be my ultimate weapon. My partner. My forever.

This will be our game.

Truth or dare.

Fuck and kill.

When I asked her the question, I knew she wouldn't answer truthfully. The anger danced in her eyes, but there was another emotion I didn't bank on. Fear. Her new desire for blood matches mine. We're on par as the perfect match. I know she wants it. And I'm here to deliver.

When I first laid eyes on the beauty, she was ten years old. At my sixteen years, I didn't know why I wanted to talk to her, but I did. She smiled at me, but her father stole her away that day before I could say hello, sending her indoors away from me. The thing is, he didn't bank on her and Meredith befriending Darick and me. He didn't realize that Eliana and I were made for each other. Neither did anyone else.

I put it down to the fact that he knew the life my brother and I would one day lead, and he didn't want his little girl caught up in the web of darkness. But she was the epitome of our world. She was born for us, for me.

When her sister was murdered, Darick and I left. We walked out, and I was never meant to see her again. So, I focused on creating a new life. I had two jobs — one with Nathan, who gave me a chance at being *normal,* and one with Oliver, who offered me the release I needed by killing those who deserved to die. And with every life I took, it was always Eliana I was fighting for. I became a force to be reckoned with, and so did Darick. Ultimately, I knew he loved her as well. And all we did was to keep her safe.

Losing Eliana took me back to a dark memory that crept into my veins. The moment my life fell apart, and I did delve head first into the life my father set out for me. Slowly, with each spade of earth that fell on the coffin as they buried my mother, I knew I had to exact my revenge on the asshole who stole her from me.

I despise my father for what he didn't do. Save my mother. This tangled web that's been woven is intricate. One snare and we all fall to the ground. Our lives have been bound together by two dangerous yet intense emotions — love and hate.

Now that I'm back for her, I won't let anything, or

anyone, get in my way.

That deep-seated need to hurt those who've hurt me, those who deserve punishment for their sins drives me forward. Eliana, Darick, and I will one day have everything. Our fathers' have built strong foundations for us to inherit, and it's time Sean relinquishes control.

I will take the little vixen beside me who's got my cock hard and make her the strongest she's ever been. Bit by bit, I want to unravel her. Like a ball of twine, I want to pull and tug until all she's hidden are revealed. Peeling away at the surface of her innocent demeanor I know is all a lie. I've seen her. The real her she hides from the world.

I've spied on her when she thinks no one is watching, but I am, always. I've seen her hunger. The desire she only unleashes in the dark, with her hand between her thighs. All the loss she's suffered has made her cold, hungry, and angry. It's hardened her. I see it flash in her green eyes. Her fire will blaze through both organizations, and she'll be the Queen. And I'll be right beside her.

I'm going to drag the darkest secrets from her mind,

from her heart. I'm going to bury myself so deep inside her she'll need to carve the flesh from her bones to get me out. I'll be deeply rooted in her veins, racing through her blood. And once she's addicted to me, I'll watch her come apart, see her mind open, and all those dark memories free themselves.

When she finally learns the truth of what happened that night, the night she's blocked out, I'll be the only thing that can save her from the fall. The night her sister died she was there. She stood in the bedroom and watched crimson liquid seep into the sheets.

She doesn't remember anything, but I do. The events of that night are burned into my mind, they're etched in my heart, and they drip like a poison through my blood. I heard her scream — loud and shrill — I felt it in my bones, and I knew it was Eliana breaking.

I walked out. I was shoved out the door, leaving her with her father who later ensured she would live her life alone. With his threat that if I ever returned, he'd have me imprisoned, killed, I couldn't risk letting him know that I came back time and again and hid in the shadows to make sure she was okay. Only, she wasn't. That night

was swiped from her memory. Oliver helped me find her medical records, and that's when I learned what was wrong with her. And I vowed I'd make them all pay.

I'm here to finally set her free. I want to cure my sweet vixen. The angel that came into my life like a ray of sunshine, that made me feel again. With her smile, she made my dead heart beat again, and I will do the same for her. She will love again. And when she does, it will be me.

Pulling my phone from my pocket, I hit dial on the number of the man who's promised to help me fix her. Oliver Michaelson.

Three rings later, his deep voice greets me.

"Asher, to what do I owe this pleasure?"

"I want you to make sure everything is set for Eliana. You said that Dillon would be able to help. I just want her to remember," I implore him.

"He's good at what he does, and I have no doubt he'll be able to do this. He's worked with CIA and FBI. At the moment, he's working for MI5 in London. With his talents, he'll be able to put her under hypnosis and hopefully track her back to the past."

"I hope so." I stalk down toward the quad, ignoring the pitiful little girls staring at me like I'm going to give them the time of day. Before I reach my Jeep, I glimpse a pretty blonde who could be the spitting image of Eliana.

She's dropped her books, bent at the waist, her ass raised, causing me to lift a dark eyebrow. I can't help my eyes dropping to the space between her legs where her short skirt, which is utter craziness for this weather, teases a glimpse of pink panties below.

"Asher, are you listening to me?"

"Yeah, sorry, something caught my attention," I tell him on a chuckle.

"You mean you saw some gorgeous pussy again?" he questions, knowing me far too well.

"Something like that, Oliver. I'll see you this weekend."

"I'll be there to liaise, and I have a job for you, if you're up for it, of course."

"I am, but my father . . ."

He sighs, knowing what I want to say. "I know. We'll sort it out."

"Thanks, Oliver." I hang up before he can say

anything more and make my way to the girl who's now standing, offering me a view of cleavage I could bury my dick between.

"Hi," she says, blushing as I near her.

"Are you okay?" I question, feigning concern for her. She nods, her cheeks darkening further at my attention. She's dressed like a slut, which makes me wonder if she takes it like one too. My gaze lifts momentarily to see Eliana walking from one class to another. Her eyes meet mine, and an idea pops into my head. Reaching for the plaything in front of me, I tug her closer and crash my mouth on hers, but my stare is pinned on the woman with the white hair and green eyes that now shoot angry daggers my way.

First point, Asher.

Remember me, vixen.

VILLAIN

Blood. Money. Revenge.

The only three things I depend on, they're constant. It's been years since I made my first kill, the most satisfying moment was when I watched a life being snuffed out.

Not, it's in the shadows where I spend most of my life. Through the anger and heartache, I've come out the other side stronger, more volatile than ever before.

I've waited and watched her for years. Spent my time planning how to best ensure she pays for what she's done, how she changed lives in one stupid moment of acting out. I could've given her everything. But she took it all away.

I've allowed myself to walk the fine line that most sane people would cringe at and play games with others' lives like cat and mouse. The thing about it is, the games

I play allow me to stay shadowed from those who seek vengeance.

The first time I took a life, it's as if a switch had been flipped. My soul charred with the remains of the man I'd shot in cold blood. It was easy. I didn't feel a thing. Why? Because they walked into my life. Two girls. Sisters. Beautiful, tempting, and too dangerous. Their presence was sickening yet alluring. It made me volatile.

Both girls were too perfect. Too alluring. I craved them in ways that left me rage-filled. But even when one left this world, the other chose *him.* I've allowed enough time to pass. He thinks he's safe now, that his plan will play out as if he was deserving of it. But he's not.

I watched and waited on the sidelines. Seeing her with him, knowing what I had to do made it easier. When I realized that she'd fallen in love with him, I allowed the cold, blackened heart that ached for her to turn to stone. Perhaps that's why I find it so easy to gut a man with my bare hands. Maybe it's how I can easily walk into a room and pull the trigger, ensuring each person never lives to tell the tale of who I am.

The sweet Calloway girls were my downfall. They

both teased and taunted until I couldn't resist. But now, if those secrets Eliana hides inside her mind are ever brought to light, the world around us will crumble.

I wanted so badly to hurt her, for turning away from me and into his arms. To see how pretty her skin looks with blood dripping in beautiful patterns. I hungered to hear her screams. To feel her claw at me while begging me to stop. To show her the one thing I never got — mercy.

My life has become routine. Each night after I'd completed a job, I would find pleasure at the bottom of a bottle and inside another nameless cunt. That is who I've become. All because of her.

Picking up the newspaper, I glare at the old front-page article from years ago when the sweet girl was just eighteen, and the rage simmers just below the surface. Now it's time to come back to life. She had her beautiful face plastered on the front page of the newspaper as the soon-to-be top graduating student at Northwestern, her name in big bold letters taunts me.

I stare at the photo—which has served me well over the past few years—for a long while before a smirk curls

my lips. She's wearing a pretty white dress, but I know she's no angel. There's nothing virtuous about her. I would know. I was the one who planned her corruption, and she fucking begged for it.

You've always been a lucky girl, but now, your time is up.

Rage fuels me as I scrunch the page in my fist. The photo now nothing but a ball of trash. Meaningless. Worthless. Picking up my Zippo, I flick the lid and spark it. The bright red flame licks the paper, and I watch it go up in smoke. Just like her life will once I've made her pay for the pain she's put me through.

Watch out, little poppet, I'm coming for you, and this time, I don't care who you love. Because when our game is up, I'll ensure you're forever mine.

ELIANA

As soon as I step out of the building where I've been called back for a second interview to meet with the professor I'll be helping, the icy wind picks up and sweeps around me like a fog. The darkness that still comes with winter is present, and I feel at home. I've always basked in the chilliness and severe weather.

I'm hoping to land this job, which will allow me not to use the money my father left me. Even though it's there, waiting, I want to earn my own way. I never wanted the organization he left behind, but when the will was read, I became the sole heir.

When I left Chicago, needing to be away from Seven Sins, I decided to come home. To a town, I knew I should've returned to years ago. Once I was saved from the dungeon along with Giana, I felt lost, angry and alone. But now that I've had time to heal, I know it's

time to take what's rightfully mine.

"Running away so soon?" Asher's voice comes from behind me. When I turn, I take in the black leather jacket, tight shirt below, and the jeans that seem to mold to his legs. There's no doubt he's delicious, and he stirs the desire that swirls in my stomach. However, along with the need that tightens my core, anger heats my blood. I don't know why I was jealous when I saw him kissing someone else, but I was. It's stupidity. I'm not some teenage girl with a crush.

"What do you want, Asher?" I question before turning and heading to my car. Sean bought me this Mercedes SUV when I returned. He said it was a welcome home gift. Of course, being the doting guardian, he opted for a hundred-thousand-dollar car without me knowing about it.

I'm about to pull the door open when I feel Asher's body pressed against mine. Students mill around, but they don't cast a glance our way. I'm not scared of him hurting me; it's the other way around actually. I could easily make him bleed.

He leans in closer, his breath on my neck. "I love

playing games, Eliana. I think you need to find some confidence in that dirty mind you keep hidden and play with me," he taunts in my ear. Without thinking, rage simmers in my gut, and I spin on my heel, causing him to step back. My arm lashes out, but before I can make contact with his handsome face, his grip on my wrist halts my movement. "Uh-uh." He wags a finger left and right like I'm a child being reprimanded. "Don't be a bad girl. Although, I'd like it very much if you took that anger out on me in other ways." His words drip lust. Heavy with a longing I recognize from boys I've fucked in the past. Sex. It's the one thing I've been able to use to my advantage. If there's one thing I wouldn't mind getting from Asher, it's an orgasm right before I slit his throat.

"Fuck off, Asher. I'm done with your back and forth. Either tell me what you want or leave me alone."

He grips both my wrists painfully, shoving me against the car, my back flush with the door. "I do enjoy when you spit fire my way, vixen," he murmurs with a sinful grin. Releasing my left hand, he reaches up, the backs of his fingers trailing a warm, electric path down

my cheek. "Tell me, Eliana. Truth or dare? Or are you too scared to play?" I don't know why he's here, why he chose me, but something tells me he's not going to let this go.

"Truth," I bite out, lifting my chin in defiance. His head tips to the side in curiosity. Ice-cold eyes roam my face, falling to my lips for a moment before meeting my green ones.

"No fun, but . . . Since you chose truth, tell me, Eliana, when you made your first kill, did you come that night with your fingers deep inside your drenched cunt?" *He knows.* I shrug him off nonchalantly, but my heart is racing, hammering against my rib cage at the question. It might seem vile to others, but for me, it tells everyone what I monumental fuck-up I am. How demented my mind is. If he really does know and he's playing this game to bring me to my knees for him, it won't work.

"You have the wrong girl there, Asher. I don't kill and tell," I grit out my response, hoping he'll drop it. But he doesn't. Of course, he doesn't.

His hand comes up and grips my throat. When he

squeezes, my clit throbs. I can't fight the smirk on my lips. I want it rough. I need it violent. And somehow, Asher knows that. He knows me. His hungry eyes dance with flames in their depths, and I find myself needing to drown in them.

"I said *truth,* not a lie."

"How would you know it's a lie?" I retort, hissing in his face, but he doesn't even flinch. He looks ethereal, not angelic or innocent. Not heavenly at all. He looks like he's from the depths of Hell. A dark angel about to drag me into the inferno alongside him.

"I know everything about you, Eliana Calloway."

"Then you should know what I do at night in my bed, stalker." My words cause him to laugh, low and gravelly, but there's something else there. He really does know.

"I do. I just wanted you to tell me the truth." He steps back then, leaving me cold as a passing breeze picks up and causes my hair to fly around my head. We're not alone, but it feels as if we're the only people standing here. The air is considerably cooler than the beautiful summer that's passed by. The way his black

hair falls across his forehead makes him appear boyish.

"How would you know? Are you spying on me?" I'm genuinely curious now. I've been hidden by Sean and my dad for most of my life.

"I'm always around, Eliana. When you least expect my eyes on you, they watch your every move." Shock leaves me speechless for a moment as he turns on his heel. He saunters away from me, and I can't help my eyes dropping to his jeans. The way they hug his ass, thighs, and calves. Heavy black boots crunch on the gravel as he reaches his black Jeep. The car jolts my memory, and I realize when I last saw it. At the Briggs mansion. He's the son, Asher Briggs.

"Wait!"

He turns, pinning me with a satisfied smirk. The dimples in his cheeks were appearing for me like a gift I didn't know I wanted, but when I see them, I find myself needing to stare at them even more. "Truth or dare, Eliana?" he asks again, but before I have an answer, he slips into the driver's seat and the engine thunders to life. I watch his car disappear, but I still feel him all over me.

Finally, I slip into the driver's seat of my SUV and plug my phone in to charge. A message from Michael flashes at me from the screen.

Michael: ***I trust school is going well. We need to talk soon***

He didn't say anything to me this morning about my plan to ask Sean for help. We trained, then he sent me on my way without so much as a goodbye. I know he's worried about me, but he shouldn't be. I'm a big girl, and I can take care of myself. He made sure of it.

I was born for this life. I was young when I found out that Daddy does things that would make a normal man squirm. I recall the day I was hiding in his library. It was the day my view of my father changed dramatically. Only, I didn't know the whole story.

The door clicks closed, and I've just made it in time to my hiding place. He never knows I'm in here when I squeeze into the tiny cubbyhole under the staircase. I've been devouring his books one by one, and instead of taking them to my room, I read them in his office. Somehow, I feel closer to him.

Since Mommy is gone, it's only Meredith, him, and me.

He's told me many times I'm not allowed to sit in his office because it's where all his important documents are hidden, but I never listen.

My curiosity is piqued when I hear footsteps shuffling along the carpet and then the creak of leather from the old Oxford sofa. Daddy will spank my butt if he found me hiding away, but I have no choice. I have to wait it out. Even though I can't see who's entered, I can still hear exactly what they're talking about. When I hear my father's voice, I shiver in fear at his words. "We don't need to do this. There must be another way."

"Find her, and when you do, take her to the compound. There's a cell waiting for her. I want her clean, dressed, and put some makeup on her pretty face. The men will need to inspect her before we get paid." I'm not sure what the stranger means, but my mind tumbles with possibilities. All of them horrific in my innocent mind. Only, I haven't been innocent for a few years. When I turned thirteen, my curious nature had me eavesdropping on numerous conversations. Mostly about Daddy hiring men to kill others, but this is the first time I've heard him talking about a girl.

"What about her family?" My father voices his concern.

"They'll search for her, but she'll be gone by the time they even notice she didn't return from school." The stranger's cold words send a sliver of rage and shock through me.

Slapping a hand to my mouth to stifle a gasp, I can't fathom the order my father has given this man. Granted, I didn't think he was innocent from doing horrible things, but this is beyond anything I could ever have imagined. My father is kidnapping a girl; someone who is going to school, someone with a family. Sadness grips my heart, squeezing it painfully as if wanting to drain the life from me.

I'll never be like him. One day, I'll find the girl he stole and return her to her family. She'll go home if it's the last thing I do. The stranger sighs loudly, then hear another creak of leather as he rises from the sofa.

"I'll find her. It won't be difficult," the stranger confirms.

"Good. We'll get paid next week if all goes well. I'll walk you out." I can't believe the confidence in my father's tone. Shuffling, then the door clicks, and I'm once again alone with my worried thoughts and racing heart. This is wrong. So very wrong. When I blink, a lone tear trickles down my cheek for the girl about to lose everything.

After Daddy died, I found out he was blackmailed into it. He was, in fact, working for someone else. There weren't any names on the paperwork I found in his office. All code names. Stupid fucking pseudonyms for vile monsters who preyed on girls. I have a list saved on my phone.

When I found the list, I attempted to kill the first one, but he caught me instead. Locking me in a dungeon, using me as his personal toy. There was no reprieve from the pain until Nathan, Elijah, and Oliver freed me.

The memory still has bile rising in my throat, burning me from the inside out. It's dangerous for me to do this, for me to dive into the sordid world again, but I have to do something. These aren't stupid men; they're conniving and dangerous. If I go snooping into these business dealings, I could get caught *again*. And that's why Michael doesn't want me to talk to Sean, but I know he will have real names of the people I'm looking for, or some way I'll get into his office and find them. Then he'll give me the name of my father's murderer.

Pulling up to the house, I glance over and spot the black Jeep Asher was driving earlier. I can't believe he

fucked with my head so much. Exiting my car, I stalk toward the door on a mission. As soon as I step inside the house, I hear his music blaring from the second floor. The song is loud. I can hear every word. "Poison" by Alice Cooper screams through the thick wooden door.

Taking the steps two at a time, I reach the landing and head toward his room. The vibration shudders through me from the other side. Lifting my hand, I knock twice, wondering if he'll actually hear me.

The music lowers, and I knock again, this time louder than before. The door swings open, and I stumble backward in shock, and once more I tremble as his scorching arms wrap around my waist to hold me steady.

"Twice in one day. Shouldn't be falling for me yet, vixen," he smirks down at me before straightening to full height.

"Sean is your father."

"The one and only." He lifts two fingers in a mock salute. His leather jacket is gone, but the jet-black tee that looks like it's painted on accentuates every dip and peak of his shoulders, chest, and torso. He's not big, but there's taut muscle hidden beneath the material.

"Why didn't you tell me?" I ask in a whisper.

Inwardly, I groan at the way this one man has me flummoxed. I'm not thirteen; I'm twenty-three years old, and this is ridiculous, but I can't stop the flurry of butterflies that awaken in my belly when the corner of his mouth quirks into a wicked smirk that once again causes my heart to race.

"I figured you would learn who I am in due time. Also, I don't go around telling every girl who wants to fuck me who I am." He stalks by me, the music still playing in his bedroom, which I steal a peek into before following him toward the staircase.

"You have a very high opinion of yourself, Asher Briggs," I bite back, earning me a chuckle. "And the girl you were kissing? Did she at least have the pleasure of your name?" He laughs, the smile on his face genuine, his dimples deepening in both cheeks, and his eyes sparkling like a mug of hot chocolate on a cold day.

"She had enough pleasure with just one kiss, vixen," he remarks, taking a step at a time down toward the kitchen. I don't know why I'm following him, but my feet have a mind of their own.

"My name is Eliana. I suggest you start calling me that." I bite out my retort, folding my arms in front of my chest.

"Oh, I know exactly what your name is, but I do prefer a nickname for a sexy woman." He leans in, feathering his breath over my skin. His comment makes me tremble with annoyance. Once we reach the kitchen, two of the household chefs are cooking up a storm for dinner, which smells delicious. Asher opens the fridge, grabs two beers and hands me one. "You're old enough to drink. Aren't you, *Eliana*?" He makes my name sound filthy with the way it rolls off his tongue.

"I'm old enough to do anything I please."

"Anything?" His head tips to the side as he lifts the bottle to his full lips. My gaze lands on his Adam's apple as he swallows a gulp of the alcohol, and my clit tingles at the sight. I need to get laid. Fast.

"Why don't you get to play the game, Asher? I mean, are you so scared of my questions?" I taunt confidently, meeting his gaze dead on. Even though my body is trembling with a mix of fear and desire, I steel myself against this God of a man.

He tips his head to the side, regarding me closely before answering. "Truth," he smirks.

"I want you to tell me everything you know about me. Starting with how you know me and why you're messing with my head." My words are confident, more than I feel right now.

He steps closer to me, his body heat cocooning me. When he leans in, I try to move back, but I can't because he snakes one arm around my waist, pulling me impossibly closer to him. His mouth finds my cheek, feathering a soft breath over the tingling skin.

"If I tell you anything, vixen, I guess it would be that soon I'll fuck your sweet little cunt until it's bleeding. I want to feel your warmth drip over my cock until I'm drenched in your slick juices," he murmurs softly, the words causing me to shudder from desire and revulsion.

Pressing my palms against his chest, I push him away, and thankfully he releases me, and I pin him with a glare. "You're an asshole," I spit.

"You're telling me if I ripped off those little pants you're wearing and dipped my fingers into your tight hole, you wouldn't be wet?" he questions, his pink

tongue flicking out, licking at his full bottom lip.

"You can try to touch me. However, I'm trained with a blade. So, unless you're ready to lose your fingers, please, go ahead," I respond easily, watching the awe on his face.

He turns to the cabinet, pulling out a silver knife that looks like it's used to slice through a steak. "Why don't we test your theory?" he says. "If you're so confident you can fight me, perhaps you'll let me test you? I mean, surely you're strong enough to withstand my taunting?"

"And what exactly do you want to do?" I question, my eyes watching every move he makes.

Asher twists the blade in his fingers, then steps closer to me. The tip of the steel presses against my flesh, right between my cleavage. "Look how beautiful your skin glows," he murmurs. The bite of the knife stings, but I don't flinch. He pushes it harder, and I know it's breaking the skin. "Crimson sweetness." Two words and he lifts the knife. My blood sits on the tip, slowly trickling down the metal. Asher places it on his tongue and licks it off. "You taste like heaven, vixen."

I step closer to him then, my face in his. "If you ever

touch me again, I'll kill you," I hiss. Turning on my heel, I make my way out of the kitchen. I'm about to turn the corner and head upstairs when he calls to me.

"I'll be here every night and day."

I choose to ignore him and head to my bedroom where I can think without his intoxicating scent of spice and smoke. I haven't seen him with a cigarette, but I can smell it on his skin, and I'll be damned because it has me wanting to inhale more of it. More of him. And I know I'm fucked.

ASHER

All my life I've known that Eliana Calloway could bring me to my knees. She did it when I was seventeen, and she was merely thirteen, and even now, eleven years later, I'm still hooked like a fucking fish. And all she has to do is pin me with a glare, and I'm ready to do her bidding. Even though she can't remember me yet.

Pushing my bedroom door open, I stalk into my inner sanctum and revel in the silence for a moment before the next song blares to life. All I wanted to do was fuck her. To take her and make her remember everything while my dick was down her throat and my seed was spilling over her tongue. But I know scaring her away won't win me any points. No. I have to take it slow with her.

"Asher." A voice and knock alert me of my father on the other side of the door. When I pull it open, I meet the

matching dark brown eyes that stare back at me in my reflection every day.

"Dad." I nod, stepping aside so he can enter. Having him in here is strange. I've not been home for long, but I knew it would be tense with us both under the same roof.

"How is Chicago?" he asks as if he doesn't know. He keeps tabs on me like I'm a kid about to run rogue through the city.

"Good. I leave on Friday again," I tell him something he already knows. All my life there's been a need to prove myself to him. To explain why I do things. Even as an adult, I feel like a child who's being admonished.

"Yes, so I've heard. Is there a reason why you came back?" he asks, his gaze boring into me. If he knew the real purpose of why I'm so attached to Eliana, I'd be dropped at the bottom of the ocean with concrete shoes. The secret was mine and Darick's to keep. He ensured we'd never be able to tell her, but I found a loophole. Soon, she'll know what kind of monster she's been living in the same house with.

"She's beautiful." I shrug. Attempting to school

my features, I don't turn to meet his eyes. They're penetrating. I know because I have done the same to so many. We have a way of looking at people that can rip out their soul with a single glance.

"And you're interested in her again?"

"I'm intrigued. I'd like to see how well she handles a weapon. Perhaps I can take her down in a fight. She could be an asset with her personality." It's true, and he knows it. That's why he's kept her here. If only she knew that she was a pawn in a much larger game.

An innocent girl shaken from her world. Thrown to the wolves like bait, and here I am, one of them ready to tear the flesh from her beautiful bones. I want that. I crave to see what lurks below the porcelain surface. To devour her inch by incredible inch.

Her flavor has always been on my tongue. When I kissed her all those years ago, she was the only thing I'd ever wanted to have over and over again. I've fucked others. I've been inside many women, but it was always her.

"Perhaps you can take her on a job with you?" Pivoting, I meet my father's gaze, the master at all

games. I learned from him. I watched him over the years as he pushed and pulled, prodded people to get what he wanted.

"Would you allow her into my care?" He watches me for a moment, and I'm sure he's going to refuse me. With what hangs over his head, I don't think my father trusts me or Darick around her, but then he shocks the shit out of me by nodding.

"Why not? You're a good fighter. A Briggs. Do you think you'd be able to handle her?" I nod. "Then perhaps you should take her along on Friday. I'm sure she'd enjoy putting her talents to good use." He seems calm as he says this, but I know my father. There's nothing about this that would keep him calm. He's kept Eliana locked up in this town and this house for far too long just to let her go.

"Sure. If you don't mind?" I'm wary as he makes his way to the door. His hand on the doorknob, he twists and pulls the door open. I wait for an answer, and it looks like I won't get one until he turns to me and smiles.

"As long as you keep her mind locked up, you can take her anywhere, Asher." It's a warning. He leaves me

staring at the entrance to my bedroom as I ponder his words. Yes, there was definitely a threat in there. *Don't let her remember.* But that's what my plan is banking on.

I'm sorry, Dad, but this time I can't obey. This time, I'll go against everything I stand for because it's time you paid for your sins.

A vibration drags me from my morbid thoughts, and I find my phone lit up with a call. My brother's name pops up on screen. I haven't spoken to Darick in a few months. We've never gotten along, but something tells me he's heard I'm back.

"Hey, man," I answer.

Each time I've been in trouble, he would be the one to bail me out in more ways than one. When I got on the flight to Chicago, I didn't look back, and neither did he. But once my father opened another office, he broke apart our camaraderie, and we'd been forced to give up the friendship that seemed to linger under the jealousy and envy. Darick had always been our father's favorite, and that bothered me. But it was his love for Ellie that angered me more than anything.

The moment I left, I regretted walking away from

her. But I had no choice. If I ever came back while her father was alive, I'd been arrested, or worse, killed. I turned around that night and walked out. I didn't dare look at her. I knew if I'd have seen Eliana standing there with her eyes filled with tears, I would never have gone, and I would've fucked up her life as well as mine.

She needed time.

Her mind was broken. There wasn't anything I could do, and if I'd have stayed, my father would've ensured that both Darick and I never saw the light of day. So, I started working for him in London. Made him even more money than he already has. I got on the private plane and left for a new life.

Only, whenever I did anything remotely exciting, the first person I wanted to tell was her. I forgave her father for wanting me gone. He believed the lies he was fed. The four children to two powerful men all lost their lives that day. Everything that was good was ripped from us. Our paths changed dramatically.

Darick wanted her as much as I did. We'd been in a competition to win her attention, and even though we both had her affection, it was always me who had her

heart. She loved me, and I loved her. He was a friend to her, but she would never feel for him what she does for me, and that must've burned him.

We went our separate ways, harboring anger and hatred, but it wasn't for each other. It was always for one man; the one person who could've come clean — my father. His sick need was what drove us apart. The memory still causes me to shudder. The image that's emblazoned on my mind only cements the need to see him pay.

He told me love was a useless emotion. But something about Eliana made me disbelieve his words. It's never easy to allow someone in. To let them claw their way into your chest, but I did. I gave myself to her freely, and she burrowed her way into my heart before I knew what was happening. We were young, stupid, and now we're too old ever to go back. Eliana Calloway has brought about emotions inside me that I've never felt with anyone else — love, hate, anger, jealousy, and pure rage.

I would kill for her. And I know soon, I may have to.

"Maybe next time then?" I ask. She steps closer, leaning up on her tiptoes and planting a kiss on my cheek, which has a smattering of stubble.

"You're ticklish. You should shave." She giggles.

"I heard girls preferred when there's a bit of friction between their legs," I offer with a cocky wink, which turns her cheeks bright red.

Shaking my head from the memory, I can't help feeling guilty at my need for her, but it was more than that. We were always more than what was perceived. My emotions were a minefield when it came to Eliana. I craved her, hungered for her. And even that day, all I wanted to do was take her to the forest and make her scream my name. I know I'm an asshole, that's no secret. But I've waited for her until she is ready. And I know, I would've waited forever.

ELIANA

My alarm's shrill melody drags me from a dream of the raven-haired, brown-eyed God that's one floor below me. After I walked out of the kitchen yesterday, I haven't laid eyes on him again. I did hear his Jeep start, and I watched the taillights glowing down the driveway at ten last night. Something tells me he either went to meet a girl or was up to something I'd not want to know about.

Pushing off the bed, I pad over to my bathroom, as it's hidden behind two mirrored doors which looks like a closet if you weren't looking closely. The sunlight streams through the window, reminding me that I have an early exam and I need to get my hustle on.

Turning on the shower, I brush my teeth while I wait for the water to heat up. My hair is a bird's nest of snowy tangles and I groan at the thought of having to wash and

style it, especially since I'm already running late.

I step into the shower and allow the scorching spray to hit tiny pins and needles into my skin. The prickles ease my tension, but as soon as my eyes close, there's only one man on my mind. I pick up the soap and lather up my skin, feeling the silkiness from the suds as I trail my fingers over my flesh.

The water runs cold before I realize I've been lost in memories. Opening my eyes, I turn off the shower and step out into the chilly bathroom. Grabbing a towel, I wrap it around me with my mind still reeling from the sexy asshole who thinks he can play games with me.

It's been a long time since someone's challenged me. I'm not used to someone like him being in my orbit, someone who affects me to the point of stupidity. Being as close to me as Asher was, I should still hold onto a semblance of control, but somehow, he breaks that down. And I wonder what else he'll break. There is a chemistry that sizzles between us, and I know he felt it too.

I need to get out of this house. Living in the same space as Asher Briggs will not be good for me. It's time for me to go home. I'm a Calloway, and even though

Asher's father cared for me for four years like I was his daughter, I want to take responsibility for the wealth my dad left me.

Sean took me in when he didn't have to. It's time for me to move out of his house and go back to the Calloway estate. It's been left abandoned since Dad died because I couldn't face going back there. The memories were too much for me to handle, but I'm stronger now. I'm ready.

I recall the visit from Sean the day of the funeral.

"Eliana." The familiar voice that used to call me pumpkin while I ran around and chased Meredith when she was still alive comes from behind me. I remember him clearly. My father's best friend. Confidant. They worked together and went out together. Both their wives passed on, leaving them to live life alone. They were closer, almost like brothers, rather than friends.

"Sean, thank you for coming to the funeral. I know Dad would've been pouring you a drink by now. Shall I get you one?" I ask, offering him a small smile. His eyes, the color of a deep brown forest, stare at me for a moment.

"No, thank you. I'm here to offer you something I think

you'll need."

"What is that?" I ask, my curiosity piqued like I was as a child. Even now, at seventeen, I still have a mind greedy for knowledge. Wanting to know more than sometimes I should.

"Your father spoke to me long ago, when Meredith . . ." His words trail off as he shakes his head in sadness, and I know what he wants to say, when my sister died. "Anyway, he asked me to watch over you if anything were to ever happen to him."

"So, I'm meant to live in your house?" I question. He smiles, his eyes crinkle in the corners as he regards me.

"Yes. My sons are both out of the house. They work for me in different cities. The house is empty besides the staff. I'd like to have a daughter there. Perhaps Michael can train you . . . if you'd like to, of course."

Deep in my gut where the anger swirls for my father's murderer, whoever he may be, I think of training, and I can't help smiling. A vicious predator is pacing the cage of my ribs. It hisses and claws at me, wanting to be uncaged. To be set free. If ever that happens again, I doubt I'll be able to lock her up again.

I nod. "Okay, I'd like that."

His grin is filled with happiness. I may not be his daughter,

but I know this man will look after me. He pulls me into a hug so fierce tears spring to my eyes. My dad used to hold me like this, like nothing in the world could hurt me if he were here, but he's gone, and I'm alone.

"Thank you, Mr. Briggs."

"Call me Sean. I'll have Michael pick you up tomorrow. Pack what you need. We'll close the Calloway mansion until you're ready to return." He turns to leave, and I watch his retreating form wondering about my new life. I don't remember his sons at all. But if he's willing to have me live with him for a while, I won't refuse. Being in this house is too painful. Too many memories. Happy and sad ones. And I know, if I'm going to be ready to get my revenge, I'll need to be far stronger than I am right now.

Making my way out of the house and down to my car, I sigh as soon as I'm in the driver's seat. As I head down the cobbled drive, I wonder if Asher will be at school again today.

My mind is scattered at the best of times, but it's when he's close to me that it's as if he's surrounding me like an intoxicating fog, and I can't concentrate. I can't

believe I've managed all this time on my own. I always pictured my years studying alongside Meredith and having Dad here to guide me in this life.

The ride isn't long, but the moment I pull into the parking lot of the college, I notice his Jeep not far from where I've parked. I don't know if he followed me, but I wouldn't put it past Asher.

"There's my vixen." The voice that haunted my dreams all last night drags me from the thoughts of my sister. When I turn to him, I pin the asshole with a glare, but he doesn't flinch.

His black hair is messy, falling into his deep mocha eyes, which makes them appear darker. It looks like they're sparkling. They remind me of warmth and safety. With a depth so dangerous if I did dive into them, I'd never resurface. Perhaps that's what I need.

"Cat got your tongue, vixen?" he quips.

"You're insufferable. I've killed men for less," I retort angrily. He smirks. Dimples peek at me from his handsome face. When he tips his head to the side, eyes blaze with hunger and the same rabid desire I noticed yesterday.

He regards me earnestly before responding. "Oh, but I do enjoy toying with you. And I'm certain that you can attempt to kill me, but you'll never get it right."

"Fuck you." I spit the words with as much venom as I can muster. He grips my arm, pulling me closer as he leans in. His peppermint- and cinnamon-scented breath, mingled with cigarette smoke, envelops me. My breathing hitches when his lips stop inches from mine.

"Speak to me like that again, and I'll ensure you're screaming in the next few seconds with all these people watching. You'll be begging me to stop, but I won't," he retorts. "Now, before you go running off like the scared little girl you are, we start our game today. Tell me, since you didn't answer me last night."

My gaze narrows, anger simmering in my stomach, heating the blood that flows through my veins. I tug my arm from his grasp. "Fine. I'll play your stupid little game, Asher, but only because I want to see how well you take to losing."

"I never lose, Eliana." His response feathers over me, sending a shiver over my whole body. The hardness of his chest presses against my soft, pliable one. Warmth.

Danger. And a sensual heat I've never felt before blankets me.

"We'll see . . . Truth." My response earns me a smirk that causes my thighs to squeeze together.

"Tell me, Eliana . . . When was the last time you let go? I mean really felt the satisfaction of what you hide beneath that pretty exterior." His words are knowing. As if he's seen me when I've killed. Perhaps he has. Maybe he's only seen me training with Michael, but whatever Asher is playing at, he's about to lose.

"I don't know what you're talking about."

"I beg to differ. You see, darling," he says, stalking around me. His eyes are burning into me as he takes me in. When he reaches my front once more, he grins. His eyes are crinkling at the edge, the chocolate brown turning to dark mocha, sparkling with mischief. "I know more than you think. And I can't wait to unleash that huntress you keep caged within."

A shiver of fear wracks through me as his words settle in my gut, leaving me breathless with anticipation of that high. The feeling that overcomes me when I feel free.

"That so-called huntress you'd like to meet, she's firmly locked away. Perhaps you should find yourself another toy to play with." Turning on my heel, I start walking away from him, but he calls out to me.

"The forest behind the Calloway mansion," he states, halting me in my stride. "Springtime, yellow flowers surrounding you." His words filter through me, past the anger I feel toward him, and a memory flits by. "Two pairs of brown eyes, and a game of hide and seek."

Spinning on my heel, I stalk back toward him, getting in his face. "How do you know about that?" The memory races through my mind, startling me. Two boys. I can't see them clearly, but I recall Meredith's favorite game. She loved hiding, and we always needed to find her.

"I told you, Eliana. I know everything there is to know about you."

"Who are you?" I ask once more, convinced that there's so much more to this man than he's letting on. My eyes bore into his, begging for something, anything for another memory of my sister.

"Eliana, I've seen you kill. Alongside Michael, who

seems to follow you around like a puppy. But he doesn't know how much you've changed from the innocent teenager."

"What?" I gasp. *What is he talking about?*

"I know everything. Remember that." He lifts two fingers, saluting me before he turns and saunters away.

"Wait! Asher," I call out, but he doesn't respond. He merely leaves me with a migraine forming.

He exudes danger. Instead of being afraid of him, I'm dying to know more. To learn what this man is doing in my life and why he's here to unleash what I've worked so hard to keep under control.

He claims to know who I am and what I'm capable of. But it doesn't make sense. How do I not remember him? Where did he go if he says he knew me when I was a teenager?

All these questions tumble in my mind as I watch him drive away. My attempt to focus is pointless because as I turn to enter the building, all I can think of are his words.

What are you doing to me, Asher Briggs?

ASHER

As soon as I pull into the garage of the house, I kill the engine and exit the car. The crunch below my boots echoes around me in the setting sunlight. Her car is in the space beside Michael's, and a surge of jealousy races through me. She's been fucking him when she should've been with me. I want to kill the fucker for touching her. And I want to make sure she knows who he really is.

I don't head straight for the house. Instead, I make my way around to the back for a moment to think. I want to walk into the house and taste her, to revel in her essence. To make her scream for me.

The sky darkens as I settle on the lounger which overlooks our infinity pool. The water is a deep blue. With the city lights coming on, it looks like diamonds on the surface. The sight is breathtaking, and I wonder if she's at her window, watching. Perhaps looking down

at me. I don't move. I sit looking out at the colors in the sky. The red and orange glow seems to set the horizon on fire. My mind is reeling with thoughts of her because I don't see him before he speaks.

"You're looking worse for wear." The words come from behind me, and I turn to find my brother leaning against the entrance of the pool house. I haven't seen him in two years, but he hasn't changed, at least from where I'm sitting.

"What are you doing home?" I ask. Rising from my seat, I saunter over to the asshole.

There was always darkness that followed him. As if he was hiding something from me, but all the years I've known him, he never once confessed. Perhaps it's just my mind playing games with me, but somehow, I don't think so.

Being younger, I've always gotten the easy end of the stick. My father didn't bother with me until I found Eliana. But Darick was still the apple of my father's eye. The favorite son.

My brother turned into a killer, clean and calculated, but he also enjoyed torture. He's dangerous, more so

than I am. He reveled in the killing and maiming, two things our jobs entailed. I wanted justice; he wanted to murder. As violently as possible.

"I said—"

"Calm the fuck down, Asher," he says, still leaning on his arm against the glass and steel door glaring at me. "I came home to see father about business, and I heard about the pretty house guest you've been stalking," he says, finally pushing off the jamb, straightening to full height.

He reaches in his pocket and pulls out a packet of smokes. Tapping one out, he offers it to me. I take it reluctantly and place it between my lips. Once his Zippo flares to life, I lean forward, puffing on the stick until the red cherry glows in the darkening sky.

"You don't need to be here to see dad for business. You've spent years emailing back and forth. So tell me, Darick . . . Did you come back here to see Eliana?"

He smirks. His eyes shine with devious intent in the dim light. He pulls the cigarette from his mouth and blows the smoke into the sky. "Perhaps," he states. Menace hangs around him. It's as if he's wearing it as a

cologne. Somehow, every woman he's come across has fallen to their knees for him, and I never understood why. He only ended up hurting them. Some emotionally, some physically.

When I was younger, I wanted to be like him. So much so that I'd follow him around like a lost puppy. The thing is, Darick hated me as a child. With all the money that the Briggs name allows us, he lost his way along with every ounce of humanity inside him. His soul has blackened to pure darkness.

He took advantage of his position within the family and turned it into something vile and sordid. He's become something that I know our mother would despise.

"Do you still hate me as much as you did when we first left?" I question, genuinely curious about my brother.

Our eyes meet, those chocolate browns that match mine. "I never hated you, brother. I spent my life keeping you and Eliana safe." His words cause me to frown in confusion.

"What?"

"Nothing." His one-word answer ripples anger through me.

"Tell me, Darick. Are you still trying to claim her as yours? Even though you know she never did love you the way she does me?" I ask him, wondering what his plan is.

He pulls on the smoke once more, allowing the grey circles to puff from his lips before he regards me. With a shrug, he responds. "I know she loves you, Asher. That was clear when we were growing up, but deep down, don't you want to see her between us? Unless you've already fed her your cock?" His voice is a low drawl as he watches my movements. A hunter. That's what my brother is.

Rage simmers through my veins, igniting my blood as it travels through my body. "I'm here to take her to London as soon as I can. I have a friend who can help her remember. Then we can finally lay our demons to rest," I inform him. I watch him for a reaction, but he gives nothing away. He inhales another long drag from the cigarette, narrows his eyes, and nods.

"If you say so, brother," he responds. The glowing

red cherry on his smoke reaches its end as he drops it on the ground, stepping on it to finally put an end to the cigarette. "My demons will never be laid to rest. I live with them daily." He glances up at me under his long dark lashes.

"What do you mean?"

He doesn't respond. Instead, he asks, "Killed anyone lately, brother?"

"No, why?"

"Perhaps I have one for you," he tells me easily. We've worked together before. But this is different. His eyes burn with anger, rage dancing in the brown orbs.

"Why don't you do it?" I ask, shoving my free hand in my jeans pocket.

He steps closer to me, taunting me with a question. "Are you scared, little brother?"

"You know I don't scare easily. What the fuck do you need?"

"There's a lot I've done since we were banned. There's a man we need to find. He has been working with father. Eliana almost got to him, but he escaped, and I have it on good authority he is one of the buyers"

He utters the vile words that has bile rising in my throat. Turning around, he makes his way back into the pool house, and I follow.

"Who is this asshole?" I question. My lips wrap around the cigarette, and I inhale a deep drag of smoke, allowing it to fill my lungs with the nicotine. Every nerve in my body comes alight with the need to get my brother out of town.

"Lassiter, but there is a problem. Another organization marked him, so he's gone into hiding," he murmurs, pouring a three-finger shot of bourbon.

"And if I help you, all's okay between us? What about when Eliana remembers that night? She'll need you too, Darick." As much as I don't want to admit it, I can't deny she cares for Darick. "What's made you change so much?"

Spinning on his heel, he glares at me. Once again, we're at opposite ends of the spectrum. Fire dances in his dark mocha eyes. "You know nothing about who I have become, Asher. You never even knew who I was when we were kids." His words are drenched in pain. Pure agony radiates through his words which causes me

to frown.

"What do you mean?" I retort, folding my arms in front of my chest. Hatred, anger, rage glow in his eyes. Nothing short of murderous wrath swirls in the depths.

"Nothing," he tells me confidently, leaning closer, and I'm tempted to punch him. To knock him the fuck out. "You've always thought I'm like Father. Perhaps I should prove you right and break her until there's nothing left, and you can pick up the pieces."

"You gave me no reason to think otherwise. You turned to his methods. Tell me how you're different?" He doesn't respond, just shakes his head with sadness clear on his face.

Without waiting for more of his lies, I turn on my heel and head out the door, leaving him in the godforsaken pool house. I hope he stays there until I can calm down. If he walks into the mansion looking for her, there's no doubt I'll kill him.

As soon as I enter through the kitchen door, I head straight for the alcohol. I need a smoke, but Father hates us doing that inside. I pull a beer from the fridge and twist it open, downing it in one long draw. Darick has

pissed me off, more than he usually does. I'm not sure what he meant about me not knowing him. He's my brother. How can I not know him?

I grab a second beer from the fridge and head up to my bedroom. I need music and my laptop. Somehow, I have to ensure that my brother simmers down. If he hurts her . . .

Shaking my head, I push open the door and immediately smell it. Lavender and vanilla hang heavy in the air as I step farther into my space. She's been here, inside my bedroom. I cast a quick glance over everything. Nothing is out of place. Which begs the question . . .

Why is she still here? What is she looking for?

I pull my phone from my pocket. Opening the app, I tap out a short message to the little killer.

Asher: ***Truth or dare, Vixen***

Smirking as the anticipation runs through my blood, I set the phone down and take a long gulp of beer. The nicotine high is slowly wearing off, and I know I'll need another smoke to keep my hands busy. They say that

idle hands are the devil's playground, and I couldn't agree more.

The vibration of my phone has a smirk tugging on the corner of my mouth. My feisty doll has responded. Swiping my thumb over the screen, I take in her words with a wide grin.

Eliana: ***I told you, I don't play games, Asshole***

Instead of racing to her room to show her how much of an asshole I can be, I tap the call button and bring the phone to my ear.

"Why are you playing with me?" Her voice is breathy, which directly links to my dick. Even though my plan is only to toy with her, I can't deny that if she were here right now, I'd bend her over and ram my dick so far up her tiny cunt she'll forever have my imprint on her.

"Don't flatter yourself, vixen, if I were playing with you, there's no way you'd be able to speak, let alone sass the fuck out of me," I tell her, chuckling when she gasps at my words. Perhaps, only when my father's blood is

dripping from her hands will she understand how well we've played the game.

"I'm nobody's *toy,*" she bites back, and I can't deny her fire makes me want her. I love the venom she spits my way, and I intend to bring it out of her more and more each time we're close.

"I beg to differ, Eliana. You've got me intrigued, and I want to play a game." She huffs down the line, and I don't stop my hand from groping my thickening erection.

"Listen, I don't know why you're doing this to me, but I really don't want to play your twisted game. How did you know about my sister's hide and seek?"

"Think about it, Eliana. Don't you remember the two friends you made as teenagers?" She's silent, too quiet. "Brothers. You cared for them," I tell her quietly.

"I . . . I can't do this," she utters. I'm about to respond when I hear the click of the line dying. When I glance at the screen, I realize she's hung up on me. *Fuck.*

Flopping on my bed, I open my photo gallery of Eliana Calloway. I palm my cock as I swipe through pictures of her on my phone. Stalking? No. Well . . .

Perhaps. But I needed to ensure I knew her inside and out. Better than she knows herself.

I find the image that always gets me off. Her eyes are the color of a forest, with greens and browns that swirl together in a hypnotic pattern staring back at me from the screen. Her full lips are pink, glistening with some shit she swiped over them, and her tits are covered by a thin scrap of white material. Which looks to be a tank top, with thin straps that I'm so tempted to rip from her body. Her skirt hits her mid-thigh, and I know that day she was wearing a pair of blue cotton panties as the wind blew the material of her skirt up and I caught a glimpse.

My gut tells me that I'll give in to the desire I have for her. I've never denied myself a good hard fuck. Soon she'll do anything I say, because when I'm done with her, I'll be her goddamn salvation, and I'll be the only thing that keeps her from the madness that wars inside her broken mind.

Asher: ***I don't appreciate being hung up on. Be careful, vixen, I'm just as dangerous as you. Tomorrow***

our game starts for real. And this time, I have a dare for you.

I hit send and turned off my phone. If I'm going to get some rest tonight, I can't be dueling words with her all night. I wonder if she'll go to sleep tonight thinking about me. Deep down, I hope I'm there, taunting her dreams.

I want to burrow my way inside her, so deep she'll never be able to rid herself of me. The only way she will ever be free is if she bleeds out on the carpet. Her porcelain skin trickling rich crimson liquid. The thought makes me harder than before. I need to get out and find a willing cunt because being around Eliana while I'm in this frame of mind will only lead to our destruction.

Sighing, I push off the bed and grab my smokes. Pressing one between my lips, I flip the lid of my Zippo and flick the flame until it glows in the darkness of my bedroom. Taking a deep inhale, I allow the drug to trickle through me, easing the tension in my muscles. Perhaps a long hot shower will calm me down.

I down the beer. But as soon as the bottle is away

from my lips, I'm craving another. None of this is going as smoothly as I thought it would. As long as she doesn't see Darick, talk to him, and as long as he stays out of my way, then I can finally finish this.

This plan is messing with my head, just like my little brown-haired doll. The need to protect her is running rife through me. Down to my veins, I feel the need to make sure this girl is safe. I'm no fucking alpha male wanting to claim her like a possession, but goddamn I want to mark her with my seed and keep her locked up in my bedroom forever.

Tugging my shirt over my head, I cast a quick glance in the mirror. The fallen angel tattoo that sits on my bicep flexes as I move. I got it when my mother died. She was an angel in this dark world. Her light seemed to shine on her three boys, but it wasn't enough to save her in the end.

As imperfect as my father is, there was something I was convinced of, his love for her. It was clear each time he spoke of her, every time they were in the same room. When he lost her, he fell into a depression so dark that the only way he could survive the years without her was

to spill blood. And now, years later, it's part of who he is. Known as one of the most feared men in the country.

I just hope and pray there's time to get Darick out of the shit he's gotten himself into with Sean. Because I know my brother, and there's no way he's back here for vacation. My father is a man people do not want to cross.

A shark.

A fucking devil.

When my father sold his soul, I knew there was no turning back for him.

I found out after Mom was murdered that there was more to her death than Darick and I had thought. And it was all our father's doing. I've come back for one thing only. It's to save the Briggs name, because when they learn who my father is, what his proclivities are, no one will fear us anymore.

The illegal shit my father deals in will shatter the organization.

There's only one person who can help me.

Eliana Calloway.

ELIANA

My body jerks awake suddenly. When I glance at the time, I notice it's just after midnight. Asher was angry with me earlier for hanging up on him, but I don't care. Even so, I locked my bedroom door when I got into bed. Knowing he's downstairs, I feel on edge. He could walk into my room any time he wants, just like I was in his space.

My body was lit with desire when I heard his deep voice when he called. He seems to be weaving himself into my life, and I still don't know why.

He didn't deny the fact that I called him a stalker earlier, which makes me wonder if he's been following me around. My bedroom is dead silent as I get up and wander into the bathroom. Even though I know I'm alone in here, I always check every corner of the small space. Splashing my face with cold water, I lift my eyes

to the mirror. In the darkness, I look eerie. My body is still tense from earlier because of Asher Briggs.

I want him.

I ache for him, but I can't explain why.

He probably thinks I'm going to give in easily. Perhaps he thinks he can fuck around with me and I'll drop to my knees, but that's far from it. Deep down, I know that he knows more. He said so himself. After all my interactions with him, he's always confessed the truth. Never once did he lie or try to hide the fact that he is messing with me. I don't know if I can trust him though.

How does he know me?

I pad back into my bedroom and flop on my bed. Staring up at the dark ceiling, I wonder if he's sleeping. If he's plagued with dreams about me like I am about him. Yes, I've been thinking about him nonstop, but mainly because there's something about him that intrigues me. A darkness that calls to me.

I wonder then where his brother is. Even though I'm tired, I can't sleep. Getting up once more, I restlessly make my way to the patio door. Opening it, I step out

onto the small balcony. The sky is black. Stars dot the darkness, glistening white pinpricks of light. The moon is hidden by clouds, which only serves to make the night more unnerving.

I glance at the pool, which is jet-colored in the evening. The pool house is bathed in murky shadows from the trees, and I wonder who Asher was talking to earlier. There was another man out there, yet I couldn't see him clearly because he kept his face hidden.

My phone vibrates on the wooden nightstand beside the bed alerting me of a message coming through. I wonder if it's Michael. Normally when he can't sleep, he calls for a late-night phone sex session. Which if I think about it, I wouldn't mind right about now.

When I reach the bed, I pick up my phone and swipe my finger along the illuminated screen only to find it's not Michael at all. It's Asher.

Asher: ***I can't wait to finally feel you again. Remember, vixen.***

I don't respond. Instead, I place my phone on the

mattress and pull my tee up and over my head. Images of Asher filter into my mind. He's incredibly handsome, and I can't deny that when I saw him this morning, and this evening. Something inside me stirred. It came to life, wanting to claw its way from my chest. My demons wish to play with his, and I wonder if they're going to drag us both down into their murky depths. This game we're playing will be very dangerous.

It's been a long time since I felt the rush of letting go entirely. For four years, I focused on learning, on changing, and I may have slipped up a few times, but for the most part, I was good. Michael told me to always focus on the job.

Michael knows why I lose control. He's the only one who's been able to calm me, but he's never been able to stop my rages. It might sound stupid to most people, but it's real. When I fly off the handle, I don't see clearly. It grips me in a furious hold, and I can't stop what I do. The only thing so far that's helped was sex.

But there are times I've lost it, and he fucked me until my mind was clear and I wasn't a prisoner to the need that consumed me.

Who knew fucking and anger went so well together?

Pleasure mingled with fury.

White hot and addictive.

The thrill of sex has become my crutch, my go-to when my rage overpowers me. But an orgasm dims in comparison to the high of feeling blood dripping through my fingers. My body heats at the thought as I make my way out to the patio with my phone. I tap out a message to Asher, wondering if he's awake, but I get no response.

When Asher asked about me letting go, I once again found my body responding to the recent memories. Nothing more than images in my mind, and they turn me molten. Something tells me he wants to meet that side of me, and I wonder how he'll be able to handle it when he does.

The darkness that slowly consumed me over the years has never fully left me. It's wrapped me in its gloomy grip, and I'm utterly delirious with want for it. It's like a voracious eagerness that sprints through my blood, and I find myself willing to do anything for it.

It reminds me of the organization that I'll soon take

over. My father hid so many things in the shadows, and I wonder what awaits me when I return. Certain things may seem one way on the surface, but when you dig deep enough, when you uproot the underlying filth, you see what really and truly lies beneath.

I may have a perfect life in the eyes of the world, but below the normalcy, I've become accustomed to showing off lies of a bloody, decaying corpse, a closet of lies and deception. It rots day by day, and soon, it will spill over onto the shiny surface.

The cool breeze picks up, causing me to shudder. My nipples harden against the fabric of my bra, and I can't stop myself from running a finger over each one, causing them to tingle and peak at my touch. A movement catches my eye, but when I glance down toward the trees behind the property, I see nothing in the darkness.

I turn and head back inside, my body trembling and needy. I lie down on my bed, opening my legs, exposing my wet panties to the door. I know there's nobody who can see me, but it's the fantasy that sends a tingle through me. A rush of hot desire flares to life and my left hand is

between my legs, stroking the wet material. I'm almost lost in a fantasy when my phone rings.

My gaze falls on the vibrating device, finding an unknown number flashing at me. Bright, taunting, teasing. I don't usually answer calls from numbers that aren't stored in my phone, but my mind tells me it's probably Asher fucking with me. Pressing the green button to accept the call, I put the phone to my ear and answer.

"Hello." My whisper is tentative but filled with need from my ministrations.

"Eliana." A deep voice comes from the other end of the line. One I don't recognize, but a voice that stokes the fire I've already started. Frowning, I sit up and glance at the door. The thin white curtain dances in the breeze, the icy air now turning me cold, yet my core is hot.

"Yes, this is Eliana," I find myself responding, transfixed to the neediness of my cunt and the deep baritone that almost seems familiar to me. I wonder what he looks like. I want to ask him, but when I hear the decadent rumble of his tone, I forget and feel myself slip into the dark cloud of lust.

"That's a beautiful bra and panties you're wearing," he says, a rasp evident in his gruff voice. My gaze snaps to the window, but there's nobody there. There is only one window in this bedroom, which overlooks the gardens, along with the patio door, but both are empty of shadows.

"Who is this?" Fear races through me as I raise my arm in defense to cover myself, but I know it's pointless if he's already seen me. "Who the fuck is this?" My voice trembles on the last word, and I cringe at my weakness. I'm needy, and I'm not thinking straight. "Answer—"

"I'd like to play a game, Eliana," he interrupts me. "I'd like to see how much of a slut you really are. You see, I know your lies. You're playing with fire, you know. A dangerous, very lethal game that little girls shouldn't be toying with," he says confidently. I'm confused, unsure of what he's talking about.

"I don't know—"

"Like fuck, you don't. Do you enjoy playing with big boys, little girl?" he questions, and I hear the smirk in his tone. "Because you'll only get hurt, but then again, I wonder if you like the pain." There's a confidence that

oozes over the line. I should hang up, but I can't bring myself to do it.

A shiver skitters over my skin, causing goosebumps to rise on every inch of my flesh. I'm wavering between want and anxiety. If he knows me . . . "I know who you are."

"You do? Well, isn't that a turn of events I wasn't expecting. And who pray tell do you think I am, Poppet?" he practically growls down the line. His voice is low, dangerous, and as much as I should be scared, I'm not. My clit tingles at the thought of him watching me, looking at my body in a hungry, almost feral way.

"Why would I tell you? Isn't this our game?" Questions tumble from my lips, but get no answer. "Isn't it?" I bite out angrily, lifting my chin in defiance as I swing my legs over the edge of the bed, I'm naked besides the thin scraps of material that cover my tits and pussy. Making my way around the bed, I tug the curtains ensuring the window is covered fully before padding to the patio door, shutting and locking it. Once everything is closed, he chuckles darkly.

"Are you shy, Eliana?" He taunts me with a low,

soft rumble that seems to resonate through me like the melody of a song. You know the feeling. When you're in a nightclub, and the bass of a song vibrates through every inch of you. That's what his voice does to me.

"Why are you hiding? If you're so confident you know me, then why are you so scared to reveal yourself?" I bite out, finding the confidence I was taught to have in a fight. I can kill a man with a swift kick to the throat. I'm also accustomed to playing with knives. I learned from the best. Slicing flesh from bone, reveling in the blood which oozes from a wound.

"You'll learn my name in good time. For now, I want you to take that skimpy bra off. Show me your tits, and don't tell me you don't want to. That little tremble that keeps racing through your body is evidence that you're enjoying my filthy eyes on you. Isn't it, sweetheart?"

I don't answer. I can't. I can't find words.

"Come on, little one. Don't you want a stranger to see those luscious little nipples?" His words filter roughly through the line. I should hang up now, but I know who it is. It's Asher. It can only be him. Perhaps I should tell him to fuck off, but once again, I don't.

If he wants to play sick and twisted games, so can I.

My mouth tilts into a small smile, and I reach for the clasp of my bra, but I don't unclip it just yet. If it's sex he wants, I can play the vixen as well. Men fall to their knees for a woman; that's why a female assassin can do so much more damage than any of her male counterparts.

"Do you like looking at me, Asher? Is this what you wanted all along?"

"I told you to fucking do something. Obey me." His words are venomous down the line. Once I've unhooked the black satin bra that cupped my full C-cup breasts, I allow the straps to slide from my shoulders. "That's it. Show me what's soon to be mine," he says. His words once again grip me rapidly, and I allow the material to fall from my chest.

"Are you happy now?" I quip, a frustrated shudder in my voice.

"No. Touch your nipples. Tweak them. Tug them until they hurt. Do it!" His commanding tone ripples through me like a stone skipping on the surface of still water. And I don't have to think about doing it, because

I'm overcome with my addiction to the high. I'll play his little game, because soon, he'll play mine. I reach for my small, rose-colored nipple. My fingers pinch it, tweaking and twisting it until I wince from the pain that shoots from my breast directly to my clit.

"It hurts," I practically moan into the speaker of my phone, which earns me a feral grunt from the other end. I want to see him. How I wish I could see if his hand is on his cock.

"It's meant to hurt. You should know this. Now, the other one," he orders gruffly, and I obey. I don't know why. I can't explain what's going on in my mind right now, but my body, my hand, and my mind are all responsive to him and his voice.

I reach for my right breast, continuing the torture of my hardened bud. I cry out from the pinch, and he chuckles darkly on the other end of the line. "Good girl. Stop. Drop your panties and go sit on the blue chair."

I glance to my left at the chair, which I didn't notice before is positioned perfectly facing the wall opposite the bed. The same wall that has a bookshelf which covers the whole area. I was in his room earlier; perhaps he was

in mine too. It's the only explanation.

"Are you going to obey me? I don't like waiting. I'm not a patient man, Poppet," he tells me in a no-nonsense tone. I try to pin his accent, but I can't. It's darker than I recall. Decadent. Rich and delicious. I want it feathering over me as he takes me.

My feet pad over to the chair that he's clearly made sure is in position.

"Why are you doing this?" I question, looking into the darkness. I don't see a red light from what could be a camera, nothing. There are no mirrors either, so I can't fathom how he's doing this.

"Because you need it. I want to play a little game, Poppet," he tells me. "A game of honesty and lies. Are you ready?" His question stills me for a moment.

"Asher, this is ridiculous." He doesn't respond. "Asher?" The name is a whisper. A plea. I'm confused, my mind is clouded, and I don't know who I need right now, but somewhere in my lust-filled thoughts, I want something, someone. Michael has never done anything like this before, never given an inkling that he's into anything more than a good, hard fuck. Deep down, I

know Michael loves me. I see it in his eyes. But there's nothing there for me to give him. No love in my heart. I'm a cold, barren murderer.

"I told you to sit on the fucking chair," my caller roars on the phone, snapping me from my daze, and I'm certain it's Asher sitting downstairs in his bedroom toying with me. I am his plaything after all. "Put me on speaker. Your phone will stay on the dresser beside the chair. You'll need both your hands for what I have in mind."

I do as he says because, at this point, I'm just a doll for his amusement. And deep down, as much as it riles me up, it also turns me on more so than I've ever been. Before I settle myself, I place the phone on the dresser and push my panties down my long legs. Once it pools at my feet, I step out of it and pick up my phone again.

I've played games before, the intimacy of truth or dare though, but it's different with Asher. It's as if he sees into my soul and knows the darkness I hide.

"Get out of your head, Eliana. You see, I like looking at girls, beautiful girls who love to tease men. They all need to be taught a lesson," he tells me like he knows me

intimately. Like we've fucked before, and I wonder if we have and I've blacked it out somehow. But I know that if I'd met Asher at any point in my life, I'd remember him. Perhaps this is one of the previous one-night stands I walked out on.

There's something sinister in his tone. Something so filthy and dark that it burns me.

"Now what?" I ask when I've done everything he said. He's quiet for so long I think he's hung up, but then a moment later, I hear his deep breath.

"I want you to spread your legs wide for me. Take one finger, your index finger, and stroke your cunt. From where your ass is on the chair, up to where that pretty clit is throbbing for attention." My hand moves for him. Obeying his order. "I want you dripping wet." I hear the gravel in his tone. It's evident. It's rough. It's pure fucking evil.

With one finger, I slowly trail the smooth slit of my pussy, from my ass up to where my clit is hidden and throbbing just as he said. He knows me. It niggles at me. Confirming that this man is indeed Asher Briggs and he's playing a dark, seductive game with me.

"Again. I want to see you glistening. Push your finger into your hole. Show me how filthy you are," he grunts, and I swear I hear him jerking off. I do it though. I work myself into a frenzy, my hips lifting off the chair. My head drops back as pleasure overtakes me. I'm filthy. I want this.

A stranger watching me finger myself, but he's no stranger at all. This is what I crave, the heat, the tingle, electric and hot, sparking through every inch of my body. It's this and the rush of the kill that make me who I am. Either I'm focused on the life draining from someone's eyes or the high of an orgasm.

Shame. Guilt. Desire.

A maelstrom of emotion thunders through me as my body tenses. I'm about to tip over the precipice of lust when suddenly his voice cuts through the black cloud of dark desire.

"Stop!"

My hand drops from between my legs, and my gaze snaps up to the bookshelf. I don't know where he is. I have no idea where the book is that holds a camera, but I wait. Silently. Obediently.

"Lift your fingers to your mouth. I want you to taste those sweet juices," he orders, and I oblige. Sucking the arousal from my fingers, I close my eyes, reveling in my neediness. His voice comes through the line harshly. "Tonight, you'll shower, get into bed, and sleep. You are not to come. Do you understand me?" he commands in a tone that tells me not to disobey. Not to question, but I'm feisty, so I do.

"But—"

"I'll walk into that bedroom this fucking instant. I'll have a knife in my hand, and it will soon be pressed against your throat. A beautiful steel blade against porcelain skin. Then, I'll gently slice your flesh to see if you bleed red or blue. And I'll do it while I fuck your throat with my cock. Do you want that?" The threat doesn't scare me. Perhaps it's because I'm too turned on to care, but all I can think of his cock in my throat. Of him making me choke on it.

"No. I . . . I just . . ."

"What? Never wanted a man before? Or never had a man want you? Or did he never stand a chance?" His words, that final question that's uttered grip my throat

as if his fingers are wrapped around me, and a memory hits me like a fucking freight train going at full speed. It slams into my chest knocking me breathless. I close my eyes for a moment and recall something I've never been able to before. A moment that silently broke me down, and once again, I'm haunted by something sinister.

"I never stood a chance. Did I?" His eyes had lost their fire. He should've known. But somewhere in the games we played, this has all turned in on itself, and I'm left with choosing.

"You always stood a chance, I just can't love you the same," I tell him. It's the honest answer. I could never lie to him. He nods. It's a slow movement, but I watch his eyes. Brown. Mocha. They're like the trees in the forest behind our house.

"No matter what happens, sweet girl, it will always be you." His words are haunting, and deep down, I know that no matter how this plays out, no matter who wins or loses, I'll have two men to love me.

When I open my eyes, I'm alone. It's so dark. I can't see anything, but there's a soft sound to my left. My

phone still lies on the dresser. The caller still there.

"I thought I lost you to the past," he says, and I hear the utter satisfaction in his tone, and I picture him with a smirk on his face. He knows. *How can he?*

"What makes you say that?" I ask as I close my legs to his gaze from a lens I can't see. Realization hits me hard; guilt grips my chest.

Pushing off the chair, I stalk toward the bookshelf, trying to figure out where the camera could be hidden. He chuckles then, and I know he's laughing at me. He's satisfied that he's taken me to that place and made me wet for him. Which begs the question. How did he know it's what I wanted? If it were Asher, he would have said something. He would have confessed.

"You won't find me," he tells me confidently, and I know I won't, but I don't stop trying.

"I will. Make no mistake, I'll find you." My words are confident as I trail my fingers over every spine I can reach. Nothing. There aren't any that could have a camera in them. Frustration bubbles in my chest.

"If you find me, it will be fatal, my sweet. I'm not a nice man. But then again, you know that. You've always

known." There's a hint of anger in his voice. A dark edge that hangs heavy with rage so palpable I feel it down to my soul. He knows me, as I apparently know him. It's in that moment something about his voice sounds familiar.

Shaking my head, I step back and respond, "I don't know you. I can't."

"Oh, but you do, Eliana Calloway. Better than you think. Now, obey my rules, and we'll play again." The line dies immediately, leaving me screaming out into the darkened room that's now filled with the filthy thing I've done. Turning on my heel, I snatch my phone from the dresser and unlock it. The unknown number sits in the list of received calls, taunting me. I can't even message him to find out who he is.

Sighing, I stalk into the bathroom attached to the bedroom. The large mirror hanging on the wall to my left reflects a woman I don't recognize. Nothing could ensure I knew who the caller was. This couldn't be Asher, so that begs the question, who knows me better than I know myself?

My phone rings then, and I wonder if it will be him again, but I see Michael's name.

"Hello," I answer immediately.

"Why didn't you tell me about Asher following you to school?" he bites out over the line. I've never seen or heard Michael so angry before.

"What?" My head is spinning with desire, confusion, and frustration. It's late, and he's calling me to have a jealous fit. This is ridiculous.

"You and Asher Briggs will not happen, Eliana. Do you understand me?" His words send rage flowing through my veins. Volatile anger shoots through me at an alarming speed, turning my body rigid.

"You cannot tell me who I can and can't speak to. If I choose to speak to him, then I will. You don't own me, Michael."

"Like fuck I don't. You may have thought otherwise, Eliana, but you're mine. Do not underestimate what I can do," he warns in a tone that has my chest gripped in cold fear.

His words are ominous. I'm unsure what's gotten into Michael, but this is not him. All the time I've known him, he's been the utmost gentleman. A mentor to me in my wanting to learn to fight.

"Let's get one thing clear. I do not belong to anybody, and if you can't get over that, then this thing between us is done. I have no one to answer to. I haven't in a very long time. And I do not take orders from someone who thinks he may have a claim over me."

"I have every claim over you, Eliana. You just don't know it yet. I wonder if your precious Asher has told you the truth yet. Ask him why he's really here. Perhaps even ask him why Darick is staying in the pool house. And ask him why they were talking about you earlier." Dizziness hits me hard, my mind reeling from the words Michael has just uttered.

"What the fuck do you mean?" I bite out, forgetting all semblance of composure. Darick and Asher are brothers, that's as much as I know. He doesn't respond, but I can hear his ragged breaths on the other end of the line. "Michael talk to me. What's going on?"

"Asher plays games with girls like you. Do you want to be another puppet on his string?" His question jars me for a moment.

Shaking my head, I deny what I know is true. "You're trying to upset me, Michael. This is ridiculous."

"Eliana, there is only one way to win this game." His voice changes from the angry tone and is now drenched with desire.

"And how would I do that?"

"Do you recall your father's last will and testament?" He questions me with a cocky satisfaction in his tone. My mind flits back to that day. The moment the lawyer read a piece of paper of my father's final wishes for me. *Eliana will be the sole heir to the Calloway estates and fortune. On her twenty-fifth birthday, she is to choose a suitor who will rule by her side.*

"Yes, of course, I do. But there is no way I'm getting married. What is your point, Michael?" I bite back over the line.

"I'm heading to Baltimore for a few days. I trust I'll see you as soon as I get back next week, then we'll discuss how I will be the suitor your father wanted for you," he says. There's a smugness in his tone because he knows that even though we've been bound by our common link, Mr. Briggs, there's nothing more between us. I don't love Michael, and he knows it.

Also, it's no secret he fucks everything with a pussy.

We're not dating, we're not exclusive, so his desire to lay claim on me is ridiculous.

"I'll be away on a job," I tell him easily. I'll ask Sean to send me off to one of his organizations because I'm not staying here when Michael gets back. "Tell me the real reason you called, Michael? Because this ridiculous notion you have of me wanting to marry you is beyond idiotic. Tell me?"

"I wanted to hear your voice," he grunts then, and I wonder what the hell is going on, but another noise on the line alerts me of something. He's not alone. He's fucking some other woman while he's telling me that I'm supposed to marry him.

Nothing burns as much as anger. It races through your veins like a wildfire catching every branch, and that's how I feel right now. I picture taking my blade and slitting his throat. Watching his blood spurt from the gaping hole I want to leave in his neck and bathing in his filthy blood. Gripping the countertop, I dig my nails into the granite, focusing on the pain rather than the anger coursing through my blood.

"I hope she's worth it, Michael. Not sure if Daddy

would have liked me to marry a man whose fucking sluts," I hiss down the line angrily. The image of my naked body being fucked by Asher while Michael is bleeding out makes me smile. I don't wait for his response, but instead, I hang up and hang my head in frustration.

I wish my life had turned out differently. My mind is broken. I've known it for a long time. Never did I admit it, but deep down, I know something is wrong with me. After my sister died, Daddy tried fixing me, but as much as I told him I'm fine, I never was.

Asher appears in my mind then. His game had me focused on him only, no anger, just desire. Perhaps he is trying to help me. But how would he know I'm broken? My medical records were sealed when I was sixteen to ensure none of my father's enemies could threaten me when he wasn't around.

Exhaustion hits me hard, and I find myself thinking about my sister. Her smile, the way her dark eyes would sparkle. Even though we were twins, we didn't look alike at all. In the dark, I made her a promise. I told her I'd never let anyone tear me down. That was the night

before she changed. Before her personality flipped like a switch and my sister went away, leaving me with someone in her place I didn't recognize.

"Eliana, you have to remember Daddy is dangerous, and some people want to hurt him and us. Promise you'll never let anyone hurt you." She looks so sad. I don't understand why, but her eyes flood with emotion, profound sadness.

"Of course. Why are you being so depressing? Nothing will happen to us. I know it won't because Daddy is strong, and people fear him," I tell her. The darkness of our bedroom seems to hide our nightly chats. No one knows that Meredith and I talk about these things. After our mother died, we grew closer than before. We do everything together.

"I know. But sometimes, people that are afraid can retaliate, and it can cause destruction." Shaking my head at my sister, I stare at the ceiling. At fourteen, we're both homeschooled by only the best tutors, but my sister reads too many scary books. Thrillers and crime fiction that puts all this in her head.

"Stop reading all your nonsense books. Pick up a romance once in a while," I tease her. She giggles. A sound I'll always

remember. "Goodnight, Meredith."

"Goodnight, Eliana."

Slipping under the covers, I stare up at the ceiling. Suddenly, I recall a moment of my sister being angry with me. It doesn't solidify in my mind, but she's venomous. Her words are spat, trying to hurt me.

The night we found her is a blur. I can't remember much about it. All I recall is me standing, staring at her lifeless body, sobbing violently. My father's arms wrapped around me, pulling me out of the bedroom, and then strangers racing through the room.

I never once went back into the room we shared as children. After that night, it started. My nightmares, my therapy sessions. It was then that I realized I was broken. A shattered soul with only my father to offer me love and support.

Asher's voice haunts my mind then. Reminding me that there's a game going on. Perhaps more than one. With his earlier call still fresh in my mind, I close my eyes, and brown eyes haunt me.

Truth or dare, Eliana?

I can hear his voice mingling with my sister's. A memory flashes through my mind. Her voice asking me to play a game. Frowning, I jolt up in bed as the memory materializes, and I remember with clarity the day my sister first wanted to play a game.

She taunted me with a game she'd become the master at. *Hide and seek, Eliana?*

The fact that Asher asked me to play a game with him isn't lost on me. In my need to have something of my sister back, I pick up my phone and type out a text to him, knowing full well that if I do lose, it will be lethal.

Eliana: ***Truth – I miss it. I want to feel free. To revel in the need to release the rage inside me. Can you handle that, Asher Briggs? What else do you want from me?***

Sighing, I check the time. It's almost one in the morning, and my body is buzzing. If Asher doesn't want me near Michael, there must be a reason. I'll find out all the Briggs' secrets. Whatever he's is hiding, I'll know soon enough. Making him trust me will be easy. I just have to give him a few secrets. Then I'll find out his.

His response comes then.

Asher: ***Truth? I want you, but I also want revenge.***

And that's how our game starts. Truth or dare.

He wants me and revenge. I wonder what exactly I have to do with it. I want to ask, but I don't. I can't help but smile at the memory of Asher holding me. The desire he elicited.

Shaking my head, I slide the drawer open of my nightstand. The photo of Meredith and me staring up at me. I'm smiling in it. The last time I ever did smile was with my sister. I loved her. I recall loving her when I was younger, but like most of my past, it's gone.

Love.

A useless emotion that grips you in its claws, rips you to shreds, then leaves you for dead. Nothing prepared me for the agony that enveloped me in its hazy fog the moment I watched coffin after coffin get lowered into the ground.

My phone buzzes, dragging me from the past, back to the present where I've become a walking weapon. No

emotion. No love. Just finding revenge for my father.

Unknown: ***Don't try to find me, and don't tell your boyfriend about me either.***

I want to respond angrily, to tell him to leave me the fuck alone. But I don't. Because I need to know who this is and why he's targeting me.

Under the covers, I feel more relaxed as the sheets cool my heated skin. I'm hidden from view for the moment, and I wonder if he'll watch as I sleep. I've never wanted someone's eyes on me until Asher walked into my life.

Asher's game is illicit. It's downright wrong, but I want more. He is an asshole no doubt, and I'm sure soon enough, I'll find out what depraved things he wants from me as we play our game.

He doesn't know that my revenge runs deep in my veins, and nothing will ease it out. As he said, he wants me, and all I want is vengeance.

The only question is . . . Will he want me after he sees how broken I honestly am?

But for now, I'll play.

I'll take his cruelty.

Why? Because I need it.

I deserve the abuse, I crave the depravity, and I hunger for the filth.

The phone rings, causing me to jolt up in bed. Asher's name flashes on the screen, and I don't have to think twice. I swipe my finger over the Icon, pressing the phone to my ear.

"Truth or dare, vixen?"

"Dare," I murmur, wanting to taunt him as he did me.

"Take your blade that hides underneath your pillow," he rasps. His voice is a gravelly rumble causing my skin to erupt in goosebumps.

I reach for the knife, gripping it one hand. "Now what?" I question.

"I want you to press it to the swell of your tits. Either one will do," he orders. My mind is awash with the darkest thoughts. What will he make me do? "I want to hear you whimper as you bleed."

"Why?"

"If you don't fucking do as I say, I'll walk in there and do it myself." His words are dangerous but so utterly tempting. When the crimson liquid trickles from my flesh, he continues. "Now take your finger, swipe up that pretty liquid, and press it on your clit." I do as he says. When my legs spread, I moan, and he hisses. My mind is locked on his voice. He growls down the line, "Now take your drenched finger and lick it clean."

Before I have time to think, my finger is in my mouth, and the line dies, leaving me gasping, dripping, and alone in the dark.

ASHER

Her challenge is there.

Once she's knee-deep in the darkness with me, I'll drag out the girl who has been hidden all these years, and she'll once again want me. Last night, my body was hot with want for her. To feel her pulse around me, but I knew I had to restrain myself. For now.

Stalking into the bathroom, I glance in the mirror. "Soon, little vixen." My reflection smirks, as I smile back. Turning on the shower, I allow the spray to heat up. Tugging my tee off, I cast a glance at the scar slashed across my ribs, just below my pecs. It's faded, but the silver glint of it when I move in the low light reminds me of that night.

Stepping into the shower, I try to wash the memory of it away, but I can't. There have been days where I wanted to return, to show her father I was the one she

wanted, but I couldn't hurt her more than she's already been hurt. Watching her fall apart from afar broke me. I knew she'd soon patch those wounds, but she still bears the scars, as do I.

Once the water cools, I shiver under its chilly spray. I turn the taps off, exit the shower, and wrap a towel around my waist. I have a lot to do today. Before Eliana gets back tonight, I need to make sure the jet's fueled, and father has confirmed our departure.

She'll be far from everything she holds dear. I needed her away from my father to ensure she doesn't follow the blind rage that overtakes her. It's the only way. Three sessions will hopefully restore her mind, and all I can do is hope and pray it works.

I know my brother will follow behind. He'll want to see Dillon. They've had a close relationship since we were kids. So close, in fact, that sometimes I wonder if there is more between the two. Granted, they had fucked girls before, sharing women between the two of them.

My phone dings with an incoming message. The jet is ready and waiting. *Here we go, Eliana.* It's all starting as I planned.

A game.

Four players — Darick, Eliana, Sean, and me.

And there will be only one loser.

I tap out a message to the vixen with a smile on my face.

Me: ***You ready for your dare, sweetheart?***

I know she won't be able to deny me because she's feisty. She's trying to prove herself in this world that's always been ruled by men. But I know she'll be the woman to bring them all to their knees. My phone rings, dragging me from my thoughts.

"Darick," I answer my brother's call.

"I trust the plan is moving along? Dad has informed me of your flight tonight," he says over the line. "If this doesn't work . . ." His words taper off, a threat hanging on the line. My brother is an asshole, but he's a man of his word.

"You said you trusted me to finish it," I tell him, hoping he'll see reason. "And I will." He doesn't need her. I do. It's the first time I've ever gotten something

Darick wanted.

"I will see you soon then, Asher." His smirk is apparent in his tone. "Perhaps we can play together, Brother. I'm sure Dillon would agree." His desire is clear. It's a promise. Dillon and Darick would love a party with Eliana and me.

His words calm me. He's let go of his anger.

Long ago, I learned that emotion is futile. It only poisons you. I let go of all mine the moment I knew I was coming back. The rage I felt toward my father may have dimmed, but what happened that night will never be forgotten. Until the day he pays.

When everything crashed around me, Eliana was the only thing that made sense. I couldn't comfort her. I couldn't even befriend her. Shoved away because of secrets, but mainly forced apart because of hate.

"Do you think she's going to want you after she remembers?" His question stills me for a moment.

"She loves me. If she knows we didn't have a choice, she'll trust us, not Michael. Oliver knows he can help her. I just need to make sure I can wrangle her to London, *Brother*." With all the frustration racing through

me, I allow it to hang heavy in my words, but it doesn't cement itself in my mind.

"Fine. Once you're over there, I'll find you. I'll be there to help. Only, if this doesn't work and Eliana loses her shit again, then it's on you, Asher. Just remember, I'll be there watching." I hang up before he can utter any more.

My mind is still on the phone call as I dress and make my way down to the kitchen. The tiny pixie is standing at the kitchen cabinet drinking her coffee. As soon as I enter the room, her gaze darts to mine.

She lowers the mug and stares at me. Her eyes are shimmering, and her long hair is loose down her back. She's dressed in a tight black dress that hugs her slim frame with black stockings that make me wonder if they're thigh highs or if I would need a blade to slice them from her body.

"My father has a job for us to complete. You're meant to be here tonight at six. Don't be late," I tell her, stalking about the space, filling a mug with freshly brewed coffee.

"What job?" Her interest is piqued. She follows me with her pretty gaze.

Shrugging, I gulp down the scalding liquid to try to take my mind off how the material of her dress curves around her delicious tits. They're a little more than a handful, and my fingers itch to maul them while I fuck her.

"Asher, what is this job?"

"You're leaving with me tonight. We're heading to the airport, taking the private jet to one of the Briggs compounds." She narrows her gaze at me. Jade-colored gems sparkle with indignation and frustration. "What? Don't you like the fact that I'll be there? Get over it." I turn to walk away but can't help casting a quick glance over my shoulder. She's so fucking perfect I can't stop looking at her.

"I'll be there. I never back down from a challenge," she finally responds to my back. My chest tightens, and I can't explain why I feel the need to protect her from the world. From this godforsaken life, but I can't allow my feelings for her to cause me to be deterred.

"This is an important job. Trust me." It's the first time I've ever come this close to seeing the real her. Not the feisty bitch she portrays to everyone around her, but

the girl that lost so much.

"Michael told me to stay away from you," she says like we're talking about the weather. My anger heightens my senses. I clench my fists. The one still holding a cup of coffee is close to shattering the porcelain in my hand.

"And what did you say?" I ask, my teeth gritted in barely controlled rage. He cannot come between us. We're finally at the end of our plan, about to ensure we both walk away with everything we've ever wanted, including the revenge for her father's and my mother's killer. If I need to end the fucker, I will.

"I told him I'd ask you what he was talking about, that I'd find out from you what was so bad, why you're here. He mentioned Darick, your brother, is here too?" Her eyes root me to the spot. I turn my body to face her fully. Lowering my arms, I give her an open stance.

"Yes, Darick is here. It's business."

"And why are you here, Asher?" She closes off, crossing her arms while facing me. I need her to trust me. If I tell her what my father did, she'll fly off the handle. Right now, she's not thinking straight, and that can be detrimental to my plan. *Fucking Michael.*

I take a few steps toward her expecting her to back off, but she doesn't. I close the distance, no longer having the control to stay away from her. Our bodies are close, too close, but I lean in, inhaling her lavender scent, almost tasting her vanilla flavor. "I told you, vixen. I'm here for you," I remind her.

"And the revenge?" With a tip of her head, her lips purse, and she narrows those greens on me. Her face is angelic, but I know what lies beneath her ethereal beauty, a darkness — profound, intense, and deadly.

Setting the mug down on the counter, my hands land on either side of her hips. She's caged in by me. An animal. A dangerous creature who aches to devour her.

When my lips are inches from hers, a hitch in her breath is the only evidence that she's affected by me. Her pupils dilate as she meets my dark stare. "I could kiss you right now. Perhaps that's the revenge I seek. Maybe it's me bending you over and eating your sweet cunt until you're gushing all over my face. Or, possibly it's me asking you for your allegiance to help me with something that could be lethal. Which of those would you like, vixen?"

Her hands lift to my chest, pressing against me, but she's not strong enough. I can see her straining in the tight dress she's wearing. I know I'm stronger, bigger.

"Maybe the revenge I seek is kicking you in the groin, ensuring that you never have use of your dick again. If you ever talk to me like that again, I'll cut off your balls and watch you bleed out all over this floor. Do you understand me, Asher Briggs?" Her harsh tone only makes me chuckle. This banter between us has me hard as fuck.

"I like a woman with fire. Perhaps you'll do just fine. And let me assure you of one thing, Eliana Calloway. The only time you'll come close to my *dick and balls*, is either when you're sucking me off or riding me with that pretty little pussy of yours." I push off the counter, turn around, and saunter from the kitchen, leaving her glaring at my back. Her stare is so harsh I feel it through the and shirt I'm wearing.

Michael is proving to be a problem. There is only one way I deal with problems — I shut them down for good. There are many times over the years I've clashed with him. He's been the bane of my life for too long.

He's not going to stop my plan from coming to fruition. He knows about the clause set out in Mr. Calloway's will. The one that says she must be married to take over the Calloway Organization. Once Michael is out of the way, and once my father has breathed his last breath, Eliana and I will finally be free.

It's almost one in the afternoon. A blanket of dark gray clouds hides the sun, and everything is set for tonight. I will leave with Eliana to find the man that's evaded my father for six months. He's been selling weapons from another supplier in our territory, and soon he'll be bleeding out, begging for mercy. That's not something I know much about, but perhaps we'll see what my little vixen likes.

Pulling up to the house, I notice her car isn't in the drive. Perhaps she's parked it in the garage.

Exiting my Jeep, I make my way toward the thick oak door with a large wolf chiseled into the wood. It's gripping a rabbit in its jaws, and I recall the painting of this scene in my father's office. Blood drips from the

dead animal, leaving a trail of crimson liquid for its family to find.

As soon as I step inside, I find the house alive with noise. Men talking, the hissing and crackling of their camera feed echoing through the vast space. Three security detail hover near the entrance. Dad must be home. Frustration niggles at my chest as I near the office door. A security guard stands at his post, almost sleepily reading a paper. When I'm close, his eyes lift to meet mine.

"Mr. Briggs, sir," he murmurs, dropping his head in greeting. When I get a better look at the man, I notice he's far older than I thought. Perhaps in his mid-fifties. Which begs the million-dollar question, why have someone so old keeping guard of my father? I could easily take him down. So could any enemy.

"Is my father in there?" I ask him. He nods, sharp and swift. "Alone?"

"He's meeting with your brother, Mr. Briggs," he informs me, which sets my body alert for a fight. Without waiting, I shove open the office door and step inside to find Darick and Sean. They could be brothers. My father

has hair white as snow, his eyes a deep nutmeg brown, darker than Darick's, but you can without a doubt see they're family. I look more like my mother, with dark hair and brown eyes.

"Ah, Asher." My father smiles. It's a genuine grin I haven't seen on his face for years. After my mother was killed, he turned within himself. Cold. Standoffish. Nothing ever made him happy, but something my brother has said to him clearly has the man lit up.

"Father." I offer a nod with a smile of my own. Meeting my brother's glare, I tilt my mouth into a smirk. "Darick." Shutting the door behind me, I make my way to the liquor cabinet and pour a double shot of my father's favorite Scotch.

"Darick was telling me he's going back to Portland tonight. Unfortunately, he can't stay long." I nod, gulping the alcohol down in one swallow.

"Yes," Darick says with satisfaction lacing his tone. "I told Dad I'll be back in two weeks though. Once the weapons have been delivered, the office will shut down for the duration, plus I'd like to take the time to see our little killer in action." I know he's referring to Eliana, but

I don't give him any more than a nod.

"She's a lovely girl," Father says, but he makes no mention of the job I'm taking her on, which makes me wary. It's been years since we've all been in the same room together, let alone talking about the beautiful Eliana Calloway.

"I must be off. I'm meeting a couple of ladies for goodbye drinks." Darick shakes our father's hand before turning and walking toward the door. When he reaches me, he leans in and whispers in my ear, "Look after her, brother. I'll see you soon." The moment he's gone, I meet my father's inquisitive gaze. He wants to know what we're talking about, what we're planning, but I can't tell him a word of it.

"I'm taking the jet," I inform him, strolling closer to his enormous black oak desk. The darkness in this room seems to overshadow anything else, and I know my father loves it that way.

"I know. Look after Eliana. She's volatile."

His warning will not go unnoticed. I know how to handle her. "I wish you'd put more trust in me, Father. She may be dangerous, but I know that there's a way to

keep her calm. To hone her skills the way they need to be."

"Asher, I have faith you can do that. We need her to keep the mindset we've ensured works. The past is over; it's done. She needs to move on from it. If she ever finds out what happened that night . . ."

His words taper off into heavy, threatening silence. That's one thing about my father. He's not an easy man to please, but there's always an underlying threat that he doesn't voice. It's a *do as I say or be killed* warning.

Nodding, I take a sip of the second shot I poured and allowed the drink to filter through me. Just then, the door to his office opens, and my little vixen walks in. She's dressed in all black. Tights that grip her thighs and calves the way I want to. Her delicious curves are hugged by a sweater that stops just below what I know is a pert ass. Her long white hair hangs in waves that look like silken thread down her back.

"Hello, Sean." Her blush when she greets my father causes jealousy to roar in my veins. A feral animal wanting out of his cage. "Asher." She murmurs my name, which makes my dick throb with need. He's ready

to play, but is she?

"Eliana, sweetheart. You're looking angelic. Come here; sit." I watch my father move like a predator. It's his realm. He settles behind the desk, creating a steeple with his fingers under his chin as he continues. "I have to inform you about something I need your help with. You and my youngest son will be heading to meet an acquaintance of mine. Asher will inform you about everything on the flight there. I trust this is okay? I've already spoken with the Dean at Northwestern. He's assured me you'll still be able to start work if you still want to when you return."

"Sean, I'm sure I'm ready—"

"You are. I've spoken to Asher, and he's assured me you're ready for more. A challenge. If you pass . . ." My father smirks. "You'll be able to do more for me. Pay your way so to speak." Rage sizzles through my veins. For him to even tell her that only serves to anger me even more. It's his fault she's here. He's planned this for far too long, but what he doesn't know is that I've made sure he won't reap any benefits from using Eliana for his own personal gain.

No. She's mine, Father.

"I suppose I'll go and pack." She rises, smiling at the man who broke her world and offered her a far darker one than she could've ever imagined.

"Good girl. Asher will collect you when it's time." She turns to leave. Dark eyes grip me in their feral grasp. The click of the door sounds in my ears, harsh and deafening. "Make sure she kills him violently," he orders. I nod. I can't voice my opinion because he'll only get angry if he knew what I really thought.

Without waiting for his response, I turn and leave him to do whatever the fuck he needs. I contemplate paying her a visit. I take the stairs two at a time. Reaching my bedroom in seconds, I slam the door shut and turn on the music system. Fall Out Boy sings "My Songs Know What You Did in The Dark," and I can't help smiling.

Once I've packed the rucksack with what I need, I head out to the staircase to find Eliana smiling at her phone. She glances up when I reach her, those green gems pinning me to the spot. I watch silently as she

shoves the device into the pocket of her jeans.

"I'm ready." Her voice is confident, excited even, and I wonder if she's looking forward to spilling some blood. I nod, stalking by her toward the sweeping staircase that leads to the exit. All the men who were milling around earlier are gone, and all that's left is silence.

Pulling open the door, I allow her to step out into the night first. "It's chilly out," she says, and I wonder if she's trying to fill the space between us with idle chitchat. I don't reply as we get to my Jeep. Once the bags are in the trunk, I slip into the driver's seat, waiting for her to buckle herself on the passenger side.

She looks so petite in my truck, a tiny toy for me to play with. Who said boys didn't play with dolls? Smirking, I turn on the sound system, causing her to jump in her seat when the loud crack of a heavy metal guitar screams at us from the speakers. Bullet for my Valentine's song "Your Betrayal" thuds through the seats as I drive down to the ominous gates with the girl I've loved since I was seventeen.

"So," she murmurs under her breath. Even though the music is blaring, I hear her loud and clear. Even in

her darkest state. I pull onto the road and turn right toward the airstrip where the jet is waiting to whisk us off to London.

The man we're going to pay a visit to has been stealing children in the UK for three years. My father, the wonderful man he is, allowed it to happen because of the money he brought in, but Eliana and I will sort this out.

"I, uhm, I like this band," Eliana says with a smile pointing at the stereo. Her eyes glisten as I glance her way for a second before dragging my stare back to the road. I nod. I'm being an asshole, but if I look at her, I'll surely stop the car and fuck her right here.

"Eliana, can you just be quiet? I'm trying to think," I bite out, wanting her to stop distracting me. My mind is a pit of fucked-up anxiety. I want more from her. I wish I could tell her that now. "I hope you'll be able to get your mind into the job," I say, gripping the steering wheel with a white-knuckle hold.

She sends an angry glare at me, and her lips part in shock. The gasp that falls from them causes my dick to throb behind the zipper of my jeans. "Why are you such

an asshole, Asher? Would it hurt you to talk to me like a fucking human being?" she bites angrily, and I love it. I revel in her rage, and I'm in half a mind to take her right here on the side of the road.

I reach out, gripping her thigh painfully. I know I'll leave a mark, but that's what I want to do. Ensure she wears my fucking bruises forever. I want her body against mine. I love seeing how much I affect her.

"Is that any way to speak to me?" I grunt, trying to control my need and anger. Restraint is not my best trait, so my teeth clench and my jaw ticks as I wait for her to respond.

"Fuck you," she spits again. My mind goes blank; my blood boils like a raging inferno as I steer the Jeep from the road, hitting the bumpy bank of grass. "What the fuck are you doing?" she screeches, holding on as the car stalls.

I turn to her, my eyes blazing with fire so dangerous if she came closer, I'd probably scorch her smooth, porcelain skin. "If you ever talk to me like that again, I'll shove my cock deep into your throat, and you'll thank me when I'm done," I hiss in her face, causing her to

flinch. Her gaze meets mine. Green to brown. Deep, endless pools of a darkened forest to the depths of the darkest coffee. We're two opposites. We shouldn't be together, but I'll be damned if I let her go.

"What the hell is wrong with you?"

Reaching for her, I grip her chin between my fingers, lifting her face so she can't look away. I want her to see who I am. To remember, but as she stares, there's no recognition. It's been so long, but I don't blame her. All those memories have been buried along with all the secrets that I'm going to help her uncover.

"I can drag you out of that fucking seat, bend you over the hood of my car, fuck your sweet little cunt until you're screaming bloody fucking murder. And you know what? I won't stop. I'll make sure I fill your body with my seed until you're dripping sticky juices all over those porcelain thighs. How's that?" I quip, leaning in farther to get a whiff of her perfume. Sweet. Floral. However, she's anything but sweet; she's all spice.

"What is your fascination with me, Asher? If anything, I'd call you a stalker and psychopath." Her words couldn't be more accurate. I am both of those

things only because she did it to me. I fell for her hard and fast, having no choice in the matter. All I wanted was her.

In the dark, she's perfect. In the dark, I'm hers, but she doesn't know it yet. My grip on her chin tightens causing her to whimper, and my dick informs me that he loves the sound.

"I think you like that. Don't you, Eliana? Do you like being watched?" Something about my question causes a desire to flare in her eyes. I want to see her come apart. To unravel, thread by thread. How I wish I could see that.

"Let's go. This is ridiculous." She huffs like a petulant child, and there's so many goddamn scenarios that fly through my mind as to what I'd like to do to her right this second. Releasing her chin, I turn to the steering wheel and start the engine. When we're back on the road, I turn up the music, ensuring she can't say anything more.

Ten minutes and she'll be alone with me until Monday. It's all the time I could get. Once the three days are up, everything will be revealed.

VILLAIN

My mind is on her.

Always on her.

My thoughts rage back and forth between taking what she owes me and ensuring she pays it in kind. It's because of her I'm in this dark place, where all I can think of is her body, the way her tits bounce when she walks, and that pretty little ass that taunts me.

She's always teased. It's girls like her that need to pay.

Years have passed since it happened, but my hatred still burns for the woman who broke the only good thing in my life. The only thing I'm focused on is revenge, but after tonight, my cock aches to use her violently while I watch her bleed all over her pretty white sheets.

She's beautiful, ethereal, but I know she's no angel.

She's the fucking devil and seeing her like that—

violent and lost in the kill—made my cock throb with yearning. My eyes were glued to her delicate fingers stroking that sweet cunt as she tempted me. Thankfully, I recorded her. I've been watching this on a sickening loop. I almost went to her. I wanted to walk into her bedroom and force my cock so deep inside her that she'll beg for forgiveness.

There were many times over the years I've wanted to take her, lock her away and make her pay for her transgressions, but I couldn't. She has tainted my life, my world, with her so-called innocence. That sweetness she exudes is nothing more than a farce, an act she puts on for the world to see.

She's an addict to the dark, depraved desires. When I'm done with her, making her watch as everything she loves is ripped away like she tore apart my world. How she broke my beautiful doll.

My darkened thoughts flit back to the desire in her eyes. I want to see it while I'm sliding into her body. While I'm fucking her, pulling her hair, choking her. I want to hurt her. To see her heart break when I confess the truth to my *Little Poppet*.

She needs to feel the same agony I've lived with for years. And I can't wait for that day.

ELIANA

The Briggs private jet is enormous. The silver glistening metal bird sits waiting as two flight attendants stand on either side of the set of steps awaiting us. Asher ushers me from his Jeep toward the aircraft. With his fingertips gently pressing against the base of my spine, the tingles that shoot through me at his touch only causes the ebb and flow between us to simmer even hotter.

I wanted him in that Jeep. When he pulled over, all I wanted was for him to take me. Fuck me into oblivion, but I have a feeling that the moment Asher slides into me, I'll never be the same again.

Once we're seated, me on the opposite end of the plane from him, I find I can breathe again. I can't be near him. When his presence looms over me, I can't think. He commands attention, but he also turns my insides molten with need. Dragging my eyes over him, I take in

his sculpted jaw, the dark hair styled in his usual just-fucked look, and those eyes that hold desire.

"Are you going to stare at me all through the flight, vixen?" he quips, not looking at me, but I'm sure he can feel my glare burning into him. His words incite emotion in me. It's always been lust since I first saw him, but as the days pass, something else niggles at my memories. As if there's more between us.

"Don't flatter yourself, asshole," I bite back, earning me a chuckle. I hate that he affects me. Even when I fight it, I can't deny it. He turns his head toward me, his gaze burning into me. The corner of his mouth tilts into a smirk so sinful I wonder if he's really Satan and I'm in Hell.

"Why do you fight the truth so much, Eliana?" His question hangs between us with more meaning than the words he actually says. My brows furrow in confusion.

"What do you mean?" He shakes his head as if he's disappointed with my answer. "Asher, if you're going to be cryptic, how am I meant to know what you're talking about?"

"Eliana, you have the truth about your life hidden

in the depths of your mind. All you need to do is unlock that cage and release them." This time, he turns his body to face me fully, giving me the whole Asher Briggs effect. It's breathtaking.

"I don't know what you're talking about. This is—"

"Look at me," he commands, shifting from his seat to the sofas on my side of the plane. The wheels spin below us as we head down the runway, and my stomach somersaults. "I really should wait to do this, but I need you to remember."

He takes my hand in both of his, holding onto me like a lifeline. As if he needs me to keep him afloat. To make sure he survives whatever we're about to do. Fear burns through me then as I watch his eyes glisten. He implores me with one look.

"Asher, I don't know what you mean." My response earns me a sigh.

"Tell me about the night your sister was found . . ." He waves his one hand in the air, not saying the word that would finish that sentence. *Dead*.

"She . . . I was in her bedroom that night, but I don't remember much of it. My mind is a blank. They said I

shut it out because of the trauma," I murmur, my mind taking me way back. That was the worst night of my life. Seeing her lying there, lifeless, drenched in blood. We're in the sky by the time I meet Asher's eyes again. He regards me with such sadness in his eyes it grips me painfully.

"What happened?"

"Why do you care?" I question, pulling my hand from his, folding my arms across my chest. His touch scorches me, making my heart beat a little faster than it should.

"Because I do, Eliana." His words are sincere as if he's begging me to believe him, to let him in. But I don't know if I can do that. Our gazes lock in a stand-off. He wants me to remember, and I want to push it to the farthest part of my mind.

"This isn't something I talk about. After that night, I spent months in therapy to forget it. Having you bring it up is not helping me. You're only going to hurt me by making me remember."

"Who told you remembering would hurt you?" Genuine curiosity laces his question. His thick, dark

brows furrow in confusion.

My chest aches thinking about the moment my life changed forever. All the doctors told me I needed to get over it, to forget what happened. Medication, therapy sessions, treatments all made sure that night was wiped from my mind forever. Even if I wanted to, I can't recall anything about what happened.

"They medicated you. Didn't they?" he says gently, realizing that I do not deny Asher an answer about my sister's death, but I can't actually remember it.

I blink a tear before nodding. "Yes," I croak out my response as tears burn my eyes. When they land on his dark orbs, he nods slowly as understanding dawns on him. "I wish I knew what happened to her, but it's a blank. There's a part of my life that's gone, and I can't bring it back."

He reaches out, his fingers gently brushing the tears away. It's the first time we've been this close, this intimate. His fingertips cause electric currents to travel through me. It's no longer just desire I feel, but his affection.

"God, how I wish you remembered me," he says

again, his words drenched in sadness that grips my throat. "Everything I did for you."

"What do you mean?" Curiously, I wait as he shakes his head.

"What if I told you I could help you remember?" Asher's question has me pondering his offer. If he can, perhaps I can finally get closure on what happened that night. I never knew why my father was so adamant on my forgetting it. Yes, my heart hurt, but she was my sister. All I wanted was a final goodbye and the truth.

"You can?"

"Yes." His confession falls from his lips, and I want to lean in and lick it up. I want to swallow it and revel in it. I believe him at that moment. He can bring back a memory that was erased from my mind. "Do you trust me?"

Inhaling a deep breath, I cast a glance out the window. The night greets me with nothing but inky skies. In the dark, that's where all the secrets lie, and I don't know how Asher will get me to remember, but if he says he can, perhaps it's worth a shot.

I turn to meet his gaze and nod. "I was taught

not to trust anyone, Asher. I want to remember. But I want something more," I tell him. My mind plays out scenarios. If he can do this, perhaps he can help me find out who killed my father.

"Anything, Eliana. I'd do anything for you." The way he murmurs those words sound like they hold more affection than a man who's a stranger to me would experience. "What do you need?" he says, sitting back, regarding me with those beautiful orbs.

"I want to find the man who killed my father," I confess, and something passes over his handsome face at my confession, a darkness that's rigid and cold.

"I can do that for you. Only if you promise to let me help you remember."

"Why me, Asher? There are so many girls you could torment. Why did you choose me?" I ask, wanting to know how I'm sitting here with him.

"Because it's always been you, Eliana."

"What do you mean?" He shakes his head at my question and moves back to his seat. The flight attendant takes our drink orders, and that's the end of our conversation.

The pretty brunette brings out drinks, setting mine before me with a smile. I watch as she hands Asher his tumbler, the swirling amber liquid trickling over the two blocks of ice.

"You'll have to tell me one day, Asher," I say, sipping on my minty cocktail. He doesn't look at me, merely nods. His concentration is on the phone in his hands, and I wonder who he's talking to.

An hour later I rise, leaving Asher in his seat, and head to the back of the jet where there are two bedrooms. I place my phone on the nightstand after checking there are no messages from my unknown sender. I haven't heard from him, and I wonder if he's had his fun and moved on.

Toeing off my shoes, I pull the thick comforter back and run my fingers over the soft cotton sheets. Slipping under the covers, I stare at the ceiling. The earlier conversation with Asher replays in my mind, and I wonder if there is something I'm missing. He acts as he knows me. But how?

My phone vibrating on the bedside table wakes me from dreams of faceless men and blood all over my

hands and clothes. When I reach for it, the device ceases its incessant ringing, and I find a message from *unknown* staring back at me. The mere thought of opening it and reading what it says sends fear jolting through me.

Sighing, I swipe my finger across the screen and tap the message icon.

Villain: ***Do you realize that your mind is a broken, tattered black hole? But do you know who really has your best interest at heart?***

I don't respond. I can't. My heart hurts from the pain I saw in Asher's eyes. He holds more than a friendly affection for me. I'm about to shut my eyes when the phone rings. I want to ignore it. I need to push the sound out of my mind and focus on the words, on the underlying confession. Because I know who it is. I realize it's him.

Picking up the phone, I answer.

"Hello." The rasp in my voice is evident, and I hear him breathing down the line. It's not loud, more like a calming melody.

"Poppet. You've been a very good girl so far, but you left. I miss seeing those smooth lips of your cunt glisten for me. Let's play a game," he says, and I can hear the smile in his tone. As if he's satisfied with this sick game we're playing.

"What sort of game? Aren't we already playing one?" My question earns me a chuckle. He's getting on my nerves, annoying me to no end. If he does know who killed my father, I'll drag it out of him right now.

"There's never only one player in a game." His words send a chill down my spine. Shaking my head, I sit up, my back flush with the headboard. "Are you scared, Poppet?" he asks with a hint of challenge in his tone. He's taunting me, knowing I'll never be able to say no.

"What do you want?" I ask him, curious as to where he's heading with this. I wonder if I'm talking to him or if I'm merely talking to myself. *What am I doing? What do I want?* My father's killer.

"Well, that's up to you. Would you like me to tell you the truth? Or would you like to take the job I have for you?" There's almost a sinister lilt to his voice, which

alerts me that this man is definitely not playing games. He wants something only I can give him. Which begs the question — how did he know I would be up for this?

"Tell me a truth," I order him easily. There aren't any other noises coming from the rest of the plane, and I wonder if Asher is asleep.

"What is your question, Poppet?"

"Who killed my father?" The words are out of my mouth before I have time to think about them. He's silent, perhaps pondering his answer. "You promised to tell me the truth."

"I did. This is my truth, Poppet. You don't want to know who killed him. Trust me, my turn. I'll give you the answers you seek upon your return," he taunts, challenging me. "After you've killed Asher Briggs." His subsequent words leave me gaping at the phone.

That's when he laughs. The sound is dark, rich, and there's something truly filthy in it. I've played before, killed before.

"I know you're with him. I dare you to kill him. You're going to break him down until he's nothing. Once you prove you're trustworthy, I'll give you the man who

killed your father. I'm a fair man, Poppet. Do we have a deal?" There's no hint of joking in his words. His voice is deadly serious.

This is not some childish game; it's the real thing.

"Answer me, Eliana. Do we have a deal?"

"He said *he* could help me find the man who killed my father. Why should I trust you?" My retort is met with a long sigh. "Tell me?"

"Because I have known you all your life. Ask Asher about your sixteenth birthday. Do you know that he and his brother were there? They were friends with you and Meredith. He knows what happened the night your sister was killed, and he hasn't told you." His venomous words are spat with anger and fury which grip me from the other end of the line.

"How do you know?"

"Ah, that is where you need to trust me, Eliana. You're a plaything to Asher Briggs. Nothing more than a doll to toy with." His words have bile rising in my throat. It burns, reminding me that I'm no longer a child. I'm now playing games with men who kill for a living. "So, Poppet . . . Do we have a deal?"

I nod. "I'll think about it. I can't trust you. Or Asher. But with him, at least I know who he is," I tell him. Even though I don't know why I have such an obsession of Asher Briggs, he's given me more than this unknown man.

"Understandable. I'll give you twenty-four hours." He hangs up then, the line dying with words stuck in my throat. Fear. I've never allowed it to enter my world. I'd always hid it in a cage locked away somewhere in my mind. Now, however, this man has dragged it into the forefront, and I know that was his intention. He wants me to be afraid of him. All I can do is wonder why.

Placing the phone on the nightstand, I push off the bed and head into the small bathroom attached to the room. I stand there staring at my reflection in the small mirror on the wall. I'm tired. My eyes glisten with tears of frustration and anger.

Sighing, I grab the fluffy towel and dry my face. Thinking of Asher and how we confessed truths earlier, I wonder if I can trust him. It feels like I'm on a roller coaster ride and my world is tipping off-kilter.

The room is still dark when I step back into it. Surely,

we're about to land. Picking up my phone, I notice I've only been asleep for an hour. Suddenly, a dip in the plane causes my stomach to flip flop, and I wonder if it's just turbulence or if we're finally descending. My phone buzzes then, dragging my attention to the device.

A message greets me when I unlock it and tap the icon to open the app. *Unknown.* As soon as the message pops up, a video appears. Curiosity gets the better of me, and when I press the play button. The sounds of sex filter through the speakers. Moans, grunts, and skin slapping.

The couple on screen are clear as day, but I know that deep rumble anywhere. It's Michael. The woman bent over with her face on the screen is me. But something doesn't feel right. I don't remember the room in the background. She's wearing pink, and I've never owned pink lingerie. Confusion settles in my mind as the one minute of footage comes to an end.

I'm craving a release along with truth, and my unknown caller knows that. He understands somehow that this would set me over the edge. Dropping the device on the bed, I lie back, splaying my legs. I dip my index finger into my folds, finding them slick with

arousal. My head falls back, my eyes flutter closed, and I writhe on the bed. Pinching my nipples with my free hand, I finger fuck myself slowly, torturously. My moans are all I hear until the phone starts ringing. I know who it is, and I ignore it. I continue with my ministrations, three fingers deep inside my core, drenched, dripping, so fucking wet.

I play until the ringing stops, then starts a second time. I'm close. So close. And then it happens. The edge of the cliff nears me, and I leap into oblivion, crying out Asher's name as I find release. My thighs tremble, my body shudders, and the walls of my pussy pulse around my fingers as I ride the wave of pleasure into the darkness.

When I finally come down from my high, I open my eyes and take a deep breath. My body is no longer aching, I'm no longer needy, but the ringtone that screams at me tells me he's angry. As if I can feel his rage gripping me in its fist.

"Hello," I answer using my right hand with my other still cupping my pussy.

"You're a bad fucking girl, Poppet," he growls down

the line. "Do you know what happens to bad girls?" he questions but doesn't wait for me to respond before continuing. "They get hurt for being filthy. Now, take those wet fingers and suck them clean. Did you enjoy the show?"

"Why did you send it?" I question, but he ignores me.

"Do it!" His harsh order causes me to obey on instinct. My tongue darts out, licking the wetness from my digits. The flavor of my desire is intoxicating, making me want more. I want to be filled. Fucked. I need it.

He's silent for a long while as I clean myself. I know he's there; I hear him breathing. It's sensual, sexy. It makes me want to see what he's doing while he watches. Is he jerking off? Or does he control himself? I'd love to know. I want to ask, but I don't.

"If I ever see you disobey me again, our deal is off Poppet. I assure you."

"And what if I am the one to make you pay?" I ask, my eyes closing on a moan as I listen to a grunt on the other end of the call, then silence greets me once more.

"Don't forget, in twenty-four hours you need to

make your choice."

The line dies, and once again I'm alone. But am I? Sighing, I turn over, staring out of the small window at the passing clouds. Asher failed to mention where we're going, but we've been in the air for too long to be local, which begs the question. Where are we really going?

ASHER

The cold weather chills me to the bone, but I don't move. I have the target in my sights, and I plan on finishing this job tonight. She stalks into the house, her hips swaying from side to side, luring me into the darkness with her. I shouldn't have fucked the wife of the man I'm here to kill, but she felt too good on my dick.

Moving closer, I notice she's left the door cracked. And this is why I slammed her against the wall and drove my dick into her cunt. She knows why I'm here. It's no secret. As soon as I step inside, she glances my way, and a soft blush heats her cheeks. I'm dressed in black, fading into the night, but she sees my familiar brown eyes.

"Sweetheart, I've got a meeting early tomorrow morning. Would you mind going into the office alone?" His voice comes from somewhere in the room. Her eyes

dart to him; she nods slowly.

"Of course, darling," she responds, but she knows he will not see tomorrow morning.

Killing has become second nature to me. My father's organization follows those who do bad things in good places. It's how he justifies taking lives. Instead of arresting them, which can't be done anyway, we walk in and ensure they can no longer hurt anyone else.

That may make you think my father is a good man. But he's not. He has never been. Not after what he did one night that ruined the lives of four children. Four hearts torn, broken because my father wanted revenge. I hear the footfalls of my mark walking toward his bedroom. Their house sits on two floors. The second is where I'll be heading soon enough.

"He's gone. I'm scared," the wife tells me as I enter the kitchen. Fear is present in her pretty blue eyes.

"Don't be scared, sweetheart." I lean in, allowing my lips to feather over the shell of her ear. The tremble that passes over her makes me smile. So fucking easy. "Tonight, you can ride my dick until you forget him," I tell her, planting a kiss on her cheek. Turning, I head

toward the staircase and take them one at a time. The door of the bedroom is open, and he's already under the covers.

It doesn't take long for me to reach the asshole. Lifting the blade, I smile, knowing I'll watch the life drain from the eyes of a man who thinks little kids are better than his wife. The revulsion shudders through me, and I pull the blankets from his form.

His eyes snap open. The fear in them only serves to make me chuckle.

"Who the fuck are you?" I don't respond. Instead, I press the sleek, silver blade to his forehead. "Heather!" he screams for his wife, but she won't come. She'll hide until I've ensured the fucker is dead.

Trailing the sharp tip of the blade from his forehead down over his nose, I watch the dark liquid which reminds me of a Cabernet trickle from the wound.

"Please, just take whatever you want," he begs. Pleads for his life because he knows it will end soon. Tipping my head to the side, I grin.

"The only thing I want is you, six feet under where you deserve to be." As I press the knife into the soft skin

under his left eye, the flesh breaks, and once again I'm greeted by the metallic stench of his filthy blood. I allow myself to play. I revel in it. Slicing two small arcs under each eye, I stand back and watch as he tries to reach for them. To stop the flow of blood, but he can't. They're too deep. It looks as if he's crying blood.

"Fuck, what have you done?" He hisses in anger, frustration, and fear. He moves around the room, stumbling and smacking into the door before he reaches the bathroom. The trail he leaves behind beckons me to follow. Boredom was setting in as I stepped into the sterile space and met his alarmed gaze in the bathroom mirror. I grip his face, pressing my knife to his neck.

"Goodnight, Mr. O'Connell."

His throat spurts liquid everywhere. The once white room has splatters of blood everywhere. It's messy, but I love every second. As soon as his body hits the floor, I turn and walk out. Pulling my phone from my pocket, I hit dial.

"Yeah?"

"Clean-up crew. I'm done." Hanging up, I stalk into the kitchen to find Mrs. O'Connell sitting quietly at the

table. "Get on the table and lift your dress." She moves slowly, tears streaking her face. As much as she hated her husband, she's still sad he's dead.

I have ten minutes before my crew will wipe this place clean. I lift the knife and trail it over her thin nightdress. As soon as it falls open, I'm greeted by her tits and cunt. She's the youngest wife this asshole took, more than half his age. The pretty twenty-nine-year-old woman is now a wealthy widow.

"Did you wear this so I could rip it off you when I fuck you?" I ask as the blade leaves her dead husband's blood on her smooth, creamy skin. She shudders as her wide eyes follow my hand. Upon reaching her mound, I press the tip into her flesh, but I don't pierce the skin. "It's such a pretty cunt. Did he make you come as I do?"

"No." The word is a soft whisper on her plump lips.

"Good." I unzip my jeans, pulling out my now erect cock. Killing turns me on. Perhaps I'm sick, but I think everyone has a little darkness in them. I sheath my knife, then my cock. "Scoot forward. I need to make this quick." She does as I order. Slamming into her is like heaven after the kill. Her moans turn to cries of pleasure as I fuck her on the breakfast table. "You're a sick bitch, fucking the man who killed your husband," I tell

her with satisfaction lacing my tone. My hips slam into hers, my cock driving deep. She's so fucking tight. "You're going to come on my cock. Aren't you? Do you like the danger?"

"Yes, yes, please!" She cries out as her heated tunnel grips me, and I can't hold back. She's clawing at me, needy and drenched as I fill the rubber. I don't wait for her to calm down. I pull out and tidy myself up before leaving her on the table well fucked and gasping for air.

The door of the bedroom opens, and I glance up, shaken from the memory by the beauty at the threshold. So many times over the years I've wished and pictured it was Eliana I was fucking. With each woman I plundered, it never changed. When I closed my eyes, it was those jade pools of innocence looking back at me.

"You're awake," I say as she emerges from the bedroom. My cock is still throbbing from hearing her moaning and whimpering earlier this morning. I know she's been fucking her fingers, and I wonder how many times she pictured me fucking her with my cock. Because God knows, I've imagined driving into her tight little cunt.

"Yes, we've been in the air for a while," she murmurs, her eyes darting around in confusion, and I nod.

"We have been, but we'll land soon," I admit freely, waiting for her to ask more, but she doesn't. She looks beautiful, almost angelic in this early morning light. I should've told her we're heading to England, but I wanted to ensure she came without a fight.

"And kidnapping me was your plan?"

"It's not kidnapping if you came of your own free will, now is it?" I smirk up at her pursed lips and glare. She's beautiful when she's angry, so much I want her right here. I'm done waiting. "Tell me who made you come in there," I say, lifting my chin in a gesture toward the bedroom. Her cheeks flush a soft pink.

"None of your business. Tell me, Asher, why were you listening?" she huffs, folding her arms in front of her chest. It's taking all my goddamn restraint not to wretch her toward me, pin her down, and fuck her mercilessly.

"When a beautiful woman whimpers and moans like you were, there's no doubt I'll be listening, vixen. You made me hard as fuck." I rise from my seat, causing her eyes to fall to my crotch. The bulge is evident. My

cock is fighting its way out from behind my zipper.

"You're an asshole," she bites out, but there's a hint of yearning in her tone. Her pupils are dilated, and I realize she's still turned on.

"Who was it, Eliana?" I bite out through clenched teeth. Jealousy and hunger wage war inside me. "A boyfriend?" I want her. No other man can have her, and the thought of some asshole sticking his dick inside her only makes me want to murder. Kill for her. I stalk closer toward her. As soon as her back hits the wall, I lean in. Her delicate hands press against my chest, only making me growl in response. I never planned to fuck her before she learns the truth, but with her body pressed against mine, there's nothing more I want.

"Why? Are you jealous?" she grits out with satisfaction, and I'm tempted to give her honesty, but I don't. Her hands are still on my chest, burning through the material of my shirt. I wait for her to push me away. When she doesn't, I lean in, salivating to taste her skin. Her flesh calls to me. I want every inch of her marked by my hands, tongue, and I am aching to drive my cock deep inside her, but this isn't passion and devotion. This

is the sick lust between us. It's always been there. She just doesn't fucking remember it.

My lips are inches from hers, and I want to claim her mouth. Her breathing is ragged, and she smells of minty toothpaste. "You'd be so lucky, sweetheart." Our eyes meet, and I see the need in her expression. She wants this. She hungers for it more than I knew she would. This back and forth we're doing is merely the beginning. It's a dance of desire, and deep down, she longs for it.

"Asher," she whispers my name, and I can't help it anymore. I can't stop what I do next. My lips are on hers. The soft yielding of her body and the taste of her mouth undoes me, and my hands are on her ass, lifting her against my hard-on. She writhes against me, her hips rolling, taunting me with her heat.

"I want you, Eliana. I'm going to fuck you if you don't tell me to stop. Maybe even if you do," I grunt the words over her neck. My teeth bite down on the sensitive flesh, causing her to cry out in pained pleasure. My cock presses against her pussy as I grind my hips.

"Fuck me, Asher. Just take me." Her words fuel my movements. I move us toward the bedroom and kick

the door shut. Nothing is going to stop me now. I stalk toward the bed, dropping her on the mattress. I smirk at her flushed cheeks and swollen lips.

"Once we do this, there's no going back, Eliana. Do you understand that?" She nods. Pulling the leather belt from the loops of my jeans, I lean over her, wrapping it around her delicate neck. I tug it tighter, causing her to choke, but the fire and desire in her eyes tell me she likes it like this. "You want rough, baby?"

"Please, Asher," she begs. I love when a woman is so turned on she forgets where she is, who she is, and pleads for my dick. I tug the belt tighter, cutting off her breathing, and I watch with a smirk as she claws at the leather. The gurgling sounds of her attempting to pull in air have my cock painfully hard now. Her eyes roll back, and I release the belt. She gasps, her eyes glistening with unshed tears, and her mouth purses as she glares at me.

"Take your clothes off. I want to watch," I tell her, as I shove my jeans down my thighs along with my briefs. Now, settling myself in the armchair with my erection jutting out, leaking arousal for the beautiful woman getting naked for me.

Once she's bare, I allow my gaze to rake over her. I grip myself, stroking slowly, which causes her eyes to latch on to the movement. Her tongue darts out, licking her lips at the sight.

"Do you want to suck my cock?" Her eyes dart to mine, and she nods. I crook my finger, calling her over to me and she slowly crawls on her hands and knees toward me. A filthy vision of pure sex makes my cock painfully throb. She's still got my belt around her neck, and I tug on it like a leash. "Swallow me." Two words and she obeys. Her mouth slips over the crown, her tongue dancing along the shaft. A hiss falls from my lips, and her wide eyes meet mine. Nothing can compare to the sight of Eliana Calloway with my dick in her mouth.

Her head bops up and down as she takes me like she was born to do it. And she was. Eliana has always been mine. Darick enjoyed the taunt and tease of her innocence as we played our game. He would watch when I was with her, my hands stroking her beautiful teenage tits, my mouth devouring her sweet lips.

We were perfect together.

The three of us.

But Meredith never wanted in on it. And deep down, I think that's what made her go mad. She knew that even if she was there, Darick and I would never look at her the way we did her sister. Perhaps we were all sick and depraved, but it was perfection.

Until . . .

Shaking my head, I concentrate on Eliana. The soft gagging sounds of her throat cause my shaft to throb. Her eyes tear up, pretty, glittering orbs of green stare up at me. Slowly, she slides her mouth off my dick, her plump lips wrap around the tip as she watches my reaction.

Who knew the woman was a dick-sucking goddess?

I reach down, gripping her white tresses in my fist, tugging her head back. "Time to really take my cock," I tell her before bringing her face closer. Her mouth opens instinctively, and my hips lift, my shaft pressing the back of her throat. My head drops back as pleasure rockets through me like lightning striking my veins. I pull out and slam back into her throat. Opening my eyes, I watch as her body convulses below me. Pretty green eyes stream with tears. Her saliva drips from her chin

and onto her pretty tits.

I continue abusing her face, using her for my pleasure, and she takes it. She's fucking flawless. I always knew she was, but seeing her gag on my thick erection is utter perfection. I pull her off me, giving her a moment to breathe, then gripping the belt which causes her to cough and splutter.

"Is this what you wanted?" I grunt, my face in hers as I take in what a mess she looks like right now. Mascara running down her cheeks, her lips plump and swollen from the throat fuck I've just given.

She allows my dick to fall from her lips and rises. "Yes," she manages to murmur.

"Up. Bend over the bed."

When she turns toward the bed, I'm met with the sight of her slim hips and ass as she sways them seductively. She bends over the edge and spreads her long, lithe legs. Her pussy peeks at me, glistening with her juices that I'm craving to lap up.

I move off the chair. Kneeling behind her, I reach up and open the cheeks of her ass. Both tight holes taunt me. I lean in, and for the first time in my life, I taste Eliana

Calloway. It feels as if a drug has been shot directly into the vein. My blood pulses through me, heating, igniting for the girl I've wanted for so long.

My tongue darts out, licking over her folds all the way up her slit toward her ass. Every inch of this woman is intoxicating. I continue lapping and teasing her with my tongue until she's clawing the bedsheets. I dip two fingers into her cunt, finger-fucking her with slow, methodical strokes.

"Please, Asher. Fuck," she whimpers, pushing her body back, trying to take pleasure I'm not allowing. I know she wants it rough; she needs it just like I do. I crook my fingers inside her, finding the spot that sends her over, pressing against it until she's screeching like a fucking banshee.

Immediately, I pull out of her and rise. Grabbing a condom from my jeans pocket, I roll it on. One hand tangles in her white hair and I tug it roughly, causing her back to arch. With my other hand, I guide my rigid cock into her body. She's tight as I seat myself fully in her pussy. My hand grips her hip, my fingers digging into the flesh, and I know I'm hurting her. I enjoy the pain I

inflict on her supple body. It's the only way I can handle my desire that resonates between us now as if we didn't spend years apart.

All my life, I was taunted by the same thing that haunts Eliana, but I found that fucking it away helps. It quells the need to kill for a while. When the anger would become too much, I'd fuck.

I do it hard, rough, and I ensure the woman I'm with cries in pain because that's what I need to get off. I pull out and slam back in, but Eliana is different. She always has been. She's my equal in most things, and this is no different. As hard as I thrust, she pushes back. We meet in the middle of our sensually fueled connection.

My head drops back in pleasure as I pull out of her drenched cunt and slam balls-deep inside her tight asshole. The ring of muscle grips my erection, and a hiss of pleasure escapes from my lips. I hear her cries, her whimpers, and for the first time, I'm inside the woman I was made for. I'm using the beautiful girl I'd dreamed of for years. Eliana's soft cries send me into the abyss of desire that's long left me wanting, and I know this time, as my orgasm races through my body, causing my cock

to throb inside her, I'll never be left wanting again.

Her body pulses, she cries out "Fuck yes, Asher!" And I'm a goner. The blackness behind my eyelids lights up as white sparks appear. My balls draw up tight, and I empty my seed into the rubber. Next time I take her, I'll mark her inside and out.

ELIANA

"Meredith," I call her again, but she's playing her favorite game. Hide and seek. We've played it since we were little, but right now, at fourteen, we're too old to be playing childish games. At least that's what I think. "Meredith, this isn't funny anymore. It's getting late, and Dad is going to have our heads when he finds us outside after dark," I tell the darkening garden. Our place is secured like a fortress, but my father always ensures we're inside safely, especially at night.

"Boo!" Her voice comes from behind me suddenly, causing me to screech. "Calm down, it's only me." She smiles. Her eyes match the color of mine, green like the gemstones from our mother's old necklace. Since she died, Dad has kept her room locked up tight, and we're not allowed in there anymore.

"Let's go inside. I'm hungry, and Daddy's not going to be happy we're still outside," I tell her. We're only minutes apart in age, but sometimes it feels like generations.

"I wish he'd come over tonight." She giggles. "The boy with the brown eyes." Her whisper makes me smile. We've got friends next door. The brothers who bring us treats from all over the world. One with hair white as snow and the other has hair the color of the black ink in Daddy's fountain pen.

"They'll go away soon," I tell her while shaking my head. It's true. I know this because I overheard Dad and Uncle Sean talking two days ago. His sons are old enough to work for him, so they're leaving. Sadness etches itself around me when I think of Asher leaving.

"Maybe then we'll just have each other again," Meredith says from beside me as we slip into my bedroom. "Will you miss Asher?" she asks earnestly, and I nod. If there's one thing about our relationship, we are brutally honest. At times, it can be a bad thing, but most of the time, it's as if we're in each other's mind. Perhaps it's a twin thing. Maybe it's because we know how it feels to lose someone you love, and knowing that if we ever fought, we could lose the other.

"Always," I murmur to myself more than responding to her. And it's true. I'm young, barely fourteen, but I know what love feels like. Perhaps it's only young, teen, angst-filled love, but it's love nonetheless. He's been in my life for years, but I

know I'll always remember him. No matter what happens.

Rolling over, I find Asher asleep on the mattress beside me. His hair is a mess; his long dark lashes flutter over his cheeks. Day-old stubble darkens his chiseled jaw. I allow my gaze to roam over his chest. The dips and peaks of his muscles contract and tighten as he breathes deeply. I remember pieces of him like it was yesterday.

Unknown was right. Asher has been around all my life, but why wouldn't he tell me? How did I just remember him in that dream, but the rest of it is so fuzzy? The dream felt so real as I get glimpses in my mind of my childhood, but something always stops them from moving forward. Perhaps because it was a memory and not a dream. It's a recollection of something I'd been through. I've lived that moment, telling my sister how much I would miss Asher, and the moment I realized I loved him.

"Are you going to stare at me all day?" he murmurs. His voice is heavy with sleep, making it low and husky. "It's creepy, you know," he smirks, pulling me into the crook of his arm. Cocooning me, and I wonder what he's

trying to keep me safe from.

"Just wondering why you didn't tell me who you really were. And why you didn't mention that you knew my sister," I tell him, waiting for a reaction, or rather a lie. But when he opens his eyes, he meets mine with raw honesty.

"Would you have believed me if I told you and you didn't remember it yourself?" His question is valid, and I shake my head no. "Exactly. And if I told you that I once loved you as a young girl, would you have believed me?" I give him the same answer, knowing he's right.

"Why not just force me to remember?" This time I'm the one who gets a shake of his head. He leans in, planting a kiss on my forehead.

"That's why I stole you away. When you remember what happened, you need to be somewhere safe. Away from prying eyes." I pull away from him then, fear gripping my throat, threatening to choke me. Each time I've felt fear trickle through me, my mind would blank out, and Michael conditioned me to enjoy sex—rough and painful—to keep my mind clear.

"Let me go, Asher."

"No," he growls. Moving swiftly, he pins me down on the mattress. His body settles in between my splayed thighs, his hands gripping both my wrists. He's strong. More so than I am, even with all my training. His cock nudges my entrance. I'm wet and needy, and he's forceful—something I need and want. Rolling my hips, I cause him to hiss through clenched teeth. This time, there's nothing in our way. No clothes, no condom. My wet folds against his leaking shaft.

"I'll hurt you," he vows.

"Do it."

He thrusts into me in one long drive, fully seating himself, and I have to bite down on his shoulder to keep from screaming out. The pain shoots through every nerve in my body ending at my clit, which now pulses in pleasure.

"More," I beg shamelessly. And he delivers. His hips piston into me so harshly it feels like he's trying to climb inside me. "Please, Asher," I pant, my breaths being slammed from my lungs as he fucks me into the mattress.

"Bleed on my cock, Eliana. I wish I were the one to

take your virginity," he bites out through clenched teeth. He's barely holding on to the little restraint he has left. My legs wrap around his hips, my heels digging into his taut ass, willing him even closer. "Fucking mark me, vixen. Give me everything that was always meant to be mine." He bites down on my neck, his razor-sharp teeth breaking the skin, and I cry out, but the sound is lodged in my throat as my orgasm wracks through me.

Moments later, I feel his heat filling me. I can't remember our past clearly. He's so new to me, but as he slowly slips from my core, it feels as if I know him. All of him. And I've never been more afraid of someone in my whole life. Not because he hurt me, but because I love him, and I don't even know why.

He watches me as he hovers over my body. His muscles are taut with tension as he grips the sheets beside my head. Our breaths are ragged. My chest heaves against his. His skin glistens with sweat, and I want to lick it off. I want to taste everything he is if only to remember.

"Remember me, Eliana. Think about the times I've touched you, murmured to you, told you how perfect

you are as my sunshine," he coos in my ear, allowing the words to caress my bare skin gently. A shiver trickles through me, racing down my spine. Brown eyes bore into mine.

"In the forest," I say as a memory seeps through the cracks of my mind. He nods.

Pushing Asher off me, I swing my legs over the bed. An ache between my thighs reminds me I've just let him in. He's been inside me, and he doesn't want to give me the one thing I crave to remember—the truth.

"I . . . I loved you, Asher. What happened to—?"

"I was there the night Meredith died. And to be honest, Eliana, I'd rather tell you the whole truth when we're not a million miles in the air. Can't you trust me for a few more hours, until we've reached our destination?" This time he's the one imploring me. Emotion swims in the depths of his endless pools. They threaten to pull me into their orbit, and I doubt I can fight it. I want him. My heart aches when he pierces me with a stare.

"What if I want to leave once I learn the truth?" I question. We're both naked, bare to each other, and all I can think of is how beautiful he is. He takes a tentative

step toward me, reaching out to hold my hands I didn't realize were trembling. I don't know if it's fear or anger, but the emotions swirl in my chest like a storm raging in the distance. It makes me wonder what will happen when the lightning strikes and the thunder rumbles.

"Then I let you get back on the jet and fly home." It's a promise—a vow.

I allow Asher to take both my hands in his larger ones. The gentleness he touches me with is a vast difference from the way he fucked me only moments ago. His arousal mixed with my own trickles down my inner thighs as I stand before him.

"Eliana, I've loved you since I first laid my eyes on you. Today, this" — he waves his hand toward the bed that's now has crumpled sheets greeting us — "it's the first time in my life I felt alive. I've taken what I always wanted . . . you."

"At what cost?" My question stills him for a moment. "You said you wanted me and revenge. Now that you've had me, what revenge will you take?" I see it in his eyes, all the answers he wants to give. Maybe they're lies; perhaps they're truths.

"I need your help with that." He sighs, releasing me from his hold. "I wanted to do this differently, for you to find out about me, about us, when we were sitting in my home in London. But it's all gone to shit now." He turns away from me, his back tight with tension.

"Nothing's gone to shit, Asher. I just need you to let me in. It's been years since I've been around someone I could trust." My honesty has him facing me once more. The anguish on his handsome face is apparent.

"What about Michael?" My heart leaps at his question. He knows about Michael and me.

"He is my trainer and—"

"And fuck buddy?" he grunts angrily while stalking toward me, gripping my hips painfully until I'm slammed against the wall. "You let him put his dick in you. Did he take it, Eliana? Did he take what was meant to be mine?"

Frowning, I open my mouth to respond, but he shuts me up by crashing his lips on mine. The heat in that single kiss is enough to burn me to ash. When he pulls back abruptly, I miss his warmth.

"Did he fuck your virginity away?" I want to

respond. To nod, but the rage that's simmering below the surface is enough to keep my mouth closed. "Fuck!" He slams his fist into the wall beside my head, causing me to jump. The word is low and feral, growled like a ferocious animal—a strike of lightning. The threat of the impending storm as his eyes darken.

"Why? If you wanted me so badly, why did you walk away?" Anger tightens my stomach. I don't know why I'm angry or what the hell I'm doing, but suddenly, my hand lashes out at him. But as he did last week in the parking lot at school, he grips my wrist. "You're hurting me," I bite out, trying to tug free, but he's too strong.

"I'll hurt you so much worse than you can ever imagine if you ever hit me, Eliana." It's as if there are two people inside him. One waging war against the other. I want him to stop, to look at me. But his body is vibrating with unrestrained anger.

"You won't hurt me," I tell him, meeting his now mocha-colored eyes. I don't know how they can darken so much, but they do. In this dim light, it's as if the storm is here and it's about to tear us both apart.

"Yes." He drops my hand and turns away from me,

leaving me cold and alone. "I will. If you force me to, I will."

It's strange what someone's love can do to you. What their emotions can elicit. Many times, I thought I loved Michael. The realization that hits me is I was merely a toy for him to use. A pawn in a game. But who's to say I'm not one in Asher's game of revenge.

ASHER

We're about to touch down at Heathrow Airport. I spent the rest of the flight separate from Eliana because being around her made me want to tell her everything. Honesty is the only way I'll get to her, but what scares me is what she's going to do when she finally knows the truth. She's a sweet girl most of the time, but the moment she realizes what happened that night, it's all going to blow up.

Her anger will take precedence the same way it always does. The wheels of the plane hit the tarmac, and my stomach flips at the movement. Once we're taxiing down the runway, she appears from the bedroom fully clothed, and I miss her nakedness. If there's something I could forever live with, it's Eliana, and her beautiful curves bare to my gaze all the time.

"I needed time," she tells me. Her nervousness is

alluring. I want to bask in it. "All this." She lifts her hand, gesturing between us. "It's so new to me. You're a stranger, but I feel . . ." Her words taper into nothing, and I'm tempted to drag them from her mouth.

"I'm not asking you to love me, Eliana. All I want is for you to know the truth. And I promise you," I tell her, rising from my seat, pulling her into my arms. Our gazes lock in a moment of heat, passion, and agony. "I'll never walk away again. As long as I'm by your side, you'll never live in fear again. You'll never be alone again."

"Don't make promises you can't keep, Asher. This is something we need to take as it comes. There are too many things that are unknown to me at the moment," she whispers, her minty breath reaching my nose, and I want to inhale her decadent scent all day, every day.

"Listen to me. When I make a promise to you, I'll never break it. They'll have to kill me before I fail to deliver a vow I've made to you." My words are filled with raw emotion. She knows how I feel. I've told her I loved her once, but right now, all I want to do is vow that again. I can't though. Not until she's forgiven me for keeping the secret from her for all these years. I

should've fought back, told my father I wasn't leaving her, but I couldn't. I had to make a choice — keep her safe or spend the rest of my life in prison.

"It's been a long time since a man has kept his promise to me, Asher," she tells me before stalking toward the door, taking the steps two at a time to get away from me. Following her, I grip her arm before she reaches our waiting car.

Oliver steps forward, a smile on his face when he looks at Eliana. He offers her a hand, which she accepts. "Ellie," he greets in his dominant tone. "Good to see you again."

"Same here, Oliver."

"This is Dillon." Oliver turns to the younger man leaning against the hood of the car, his blonde hair blowing in the cool breeze of the winter afternoon. "He'll be escorting you to his house, I'm headed off to a meeting, and then I'll be at my hotel. If you need anything, just call."

"Thank you, for everything."

The man saunters off, and I doubt we'll need his help, but it calms me to know he is there for us.

Standing at almost six feet, Dillon is lean, with tightly packed muscle beneath a black button-up and charcoal slacks. His eyes, the color of honey, shimmer with amusement as he watches Eliana stalk before me. He merely nods in greeting, with his eyes pinned on the beauty driving me crazy.

"Let's go." Oliver and Dillon turn toward the car, and I watch as the younger man slips into the driver's seat.

"Would you stop for a second?" I tug her, spinning her in my arms until her body molds to mine. "Never will a day go by that I don't want you, that I don't crave you. Fuck, Eliana, all this time, all these fucking god-awful years, I've been without you, and you know what I thought of every fucking second?" I don't wait for her to respond. Instead, I tell her what's in my heart. "You. It's always been you, Eliana. Remember me," I once again implore her with my words, with my heated gaze, offering her my heart.

Silence hangs as heavy as the grey clouds in the sky. The rain is coming, the air thick with the promise of a storm. It brews under the surface like my hunger for this

woman. It's been there since the moment I laid eyes on her, until now. Nothing has changed. No amount of time or distance has diminished my yearning to be hers and for her to be mine.

Yes, I'm an asshole. Yes, I've fucked many women. And yes, there is a part of me deep inside that wants to see Eliana cry. To see those beautiful, sparkling tears shimmer in her jade-hued eyes. I want to hear her whimpers and moans like a song played to me on repeat. I long to feel her nails claw my back until she draws blood. And all the while, I'll be buried inside her tight cunt until she's chanting my name like a sinner in church.

"I want to remember. Tell me the truth, no more dares, Asher. This time, I want to know. I'm tired of being kept in the dark."

"Sometimes, being in the dark is the safest place, but I'll make sure you're no longer hidden in the shadows," I tell her, lacing my fingers with hers, leading her to the black town car. We slip into the backseat where Darick's already seated, talking on his phone. I knew he said he'd meet us in London, but I didn't think he'd be in the

fucking car.

"My brother, Darick," I point at the man sitting across from us, as he ends the call, and casts his gaze on my girl.

"Darick," Eliana breathes his name, causing him to smirk with satisfaction at the sound of her voice. "I didn't know you would be here."

"I figured I'd come and see the princess," he shrugs.

Dillon offers her a smile in greeting in the rearview mirror. "Ma'am." He tips his cap in a respectful nod to the woman I'm claiming as mine. Here and now. "Welcome to London," he says in his thick English accent.

"Thank you." Her grin is sweet, innocent, which only serves to make me jealous. His eyes take her in once then meet mine. He winks conspiratorially as he starts the engine.

Leaning over the seat in the front, I look at him before he pulls away. "Look at her like that again without my permission, and I'll gouge out your eyeballs and shove them up your ass," I bite out.

"Relax, mate. No harm, no foul. She's a stunner. Bet she'd love me watching you fuck her," he tells me as he

pulls out the paperwork, handing it to me before we head down the road.

I glance back at Eliana. Those green gemstones have always done so much more to me than I can ever explain. She sees my soul, my heart, my very essence.

"Are you ready?" I question her, watching her body settle against the leather seat.

She sighs, nodding. "Yes, I just want to get this over with."

I cast my eyes to Dillon. His shit-eating grin serves to annoy me further. Pressing the button on the divider, I offer him a wink just before he's shut out of our conversation.

"You two are about to explode," Darick observes when he slips his phone into his jacket pocket. "Let's see what little Ellie enjoys."

"What are you doing?" Eliana questions when I grip her hand, tugging her toward me. Her long hair hangs in messy waves, and her eyes show her exhaustion. The long flight, rough fucking, and the confession are going to be too much for her, but I need her to sleep. She needs rest before we have a job to do.

"Sit on my lap, vixen," I taunt. Her eyes roll in indignation as she settles on my thighs, straddling me like a naughty little slut. "Does it make you wet knowing how hard I am for you right now?" She nods, her shy nature taking over the sassy one. "Tell me, Eliana. You love making my dick hard. Don't you?"

"Yes," she hisses as I reach between her splayed thighs; her core hot and needy for me. Fuck, I can't wait to get her all alone in my penthouse where no one can hear her scream.

"I bet you'd ride me right here, right now. Wouldn't you, baby? Right in front of Darick," I coo in her ear, sending a shiver through her slender frame. She's petite, sensual, and I'm painfully hard. She's a temptation—a drug. And I'm an addict. "I know how many times you used to touch yourself thinking about me. I watched you. Saw you in your bedroom when you were younger, stroking your beautiful pussy."

Her eyes snap open and stares at me long and hard. She doesn't want to respond. She didn't know I knew about her naughty addiction.

I caught her once, but she doesn't remember. I was

"Do you still do it, Eliana? Do you like men watching you?"

"Fuck you, Asher." Her retort makes me lift my hips, my cock pressing against her core. Her head drops back at the movement, and I know she's still the naughty little devil who wants to be seen. It turns her on.

"Would you let me fuck you while my brother watches us?" I taunt her. "Turn around. Take off your jeans and panties. Now." She moves quickly at my order. Once she's straddling me with her back against my chest, I pull out my cock, slapping it against her drenched lips. With a grip on her hip with one hand, I use the other to push the button for the divider. "You see, baby, I can give you everything you need," I tell her. My cock slips easily into her cunt, balls-deep.

"Well, hello darling." Darick's voice comes out in a deep guttural growl. He meets my gaze, and I notice his cock in his hand, jerking off as he watches. I continue fucking the beauty, her body rising up and dropping

down faster and faster as I fill her with my shaft. She's so fucking tight I feel my balls draw up when Oliver grunts his release and Eliana squeals as she drenches my cock.

Her body trembles in my arms as she falls back. My lips at her ear whisper, "I can pleasure you in ways you'll never believe. I can give you everything, Eliana."

"Don't make promises you can't keep, Asher," she tells me, slipping off my dick, leaving me panting. Darick exits the car, allowing us time to talk. I can see him through the blacked-out window as he pulls a smoke from his pocket.

"You need to stop saying that, baby," I grit out, shoving my wet cock into my jeans. "You're mine. I'm not letting you go."

"I'm not a possession that you can own. What are you going to do? Lock me in your basement?" she quips sarcastically, with a roll of her eyes, while she rights herself, tugging her panties up lithe legs.

"Don't fucking tempt me." It's a warning because she doesn't know half the shit I can do to her to make her stay. "I've waited for too long to have you, only to let you go. Now, let's go. I'm tired." Pushing open the door,

I exit, turning to offer her my hand, which she accepts.

"Have fun back there, darling?" Dillon smirks as he pulls on his cigarette.

Eliana sidles up to him, no doubt trying to make me jealous. She presses a black-painted fingernail on his shoulder, trailing it down to his stomach. When she reaches the waistband of his slacks, she smirks.

"I always have fun when I'm getting fucked, but when eyes are pinned on me like I'm the most beautiful thing in the world, it's even better." Her words have my dick hard once more. This woman will end up killing me with mere words.

"All right, vixen, let's go." I turn, leaving her with Dillon because if I am honest, I wouldn't mind seeing how filthy she can really get. Perhaps we should share her. I know he won't mind. And the thought has my mind whirling with possibilities.

"Did you intend to leave me back there with your best friend?" she asks when she reaches me at the elevator, her light brow lifting into a beautiful arc.

Pushing the call button, I don't respond, because if I did, I'd probably have both her tiny holes filled with

mine and Dillon's dicks.

"Did you want me to fuck him?" she quips as the doors slide open and I step inside. Once again, I ignore her. We're alone once the metal doors close, and I spin toward her, pressing her against the wall. Her green pools lift to mine, fire dancing in them — desire and yearning.

"I want to hurt you. To make you feel both of us while you cry out my name. And you know how I know my name will be the one you scream? Because I'm the one that's in here." I press a finger to her chest right where her heart is heavily thrumming against my touch.

ELIANA

The touch of his fingers does things to me, things I've long ago buried. When I've been with men in the past, it's been physical, but with Asher, it's emotional. I can't explain it now. Even as his fingertips touch my chest, I feel everything sizzle just beneath the clothes I'm wearing. My skin is dotted with goosebumps, my blood running hot with need.

"I wish I remembered more. You. Us." My words are clear and confident, and I see the agony that dances in his dark brown eyes. He wants me to remember him, to love him once more. *Would my mind ever recall those times?*

"I know," he says sadly. "But I plan to remind you, Eliana. That's why I asked my father to allow you to come with me on this job because I need to do this while you're away from him."

"Why?" I question, pushing him a step backward because I can't think clearly when his hands are on me. Even just the tips of his fingers cause my mind to falter.

"You'll learn soon enough. My brother will join us as well. He'll want to be here for you," he confesses on a sigh. Darick Briggs.

"What do you mean?" I ask him, curiosity at the other Briggs brother.

He opens his mouth to respond, but the doors slide open on the top floor. Shaking his head, he turns and steps out of the elevator, holding a hand to me. I glance at it for a moment before accepting. We make our way in silence to a door with eighty-four on it in silver numbers.

He's silent while he unlocks it and allows me to enter first. A gasp falls from my lips when I step inside. I wasn't expecting it, but the living room and entrance foyer are incredibly beautiful. Furnished in dark reds, black, and charcoal, it gives the place warmth you wouldn't expect from a modern space.

I don't ask permission; instead, I walk into the living room area and take in the view of London below us. We're close to the docks, perhaps Canary Wharf, but

I can't be sure. I've never been to Europe. There are small boats docked on jutting piers contrasted by skyscrapers in the distance. Buildings are the color of ash with one prominent, blue glass building in the center of them all.

"This view is incredible," I whisper. It's low, but I know he heard me. The heat of his body is close, but he's not touching me. Perhaps he's giving me time.

"You're incredible." His voice holds a gloomy affection. When I turn to face him once more, he's standing with his hands shoved into the front pockets of his jeans. His head hangs, causing the dark locks of his hair to fall into his deep mocha eyes. He watches me from under his long black lashes, the color causing the brown of his irises to pop.

He's handsome.

Rugged, but beautiful.

A masterpiece.

"Will you tell me now? I want to know about us," I tell him, closing the distance between us. I can't stand being far from him. But then again, we've known each other far longer apparently. I reach for his face, but with lightning speed, his hand comes from his pocket

and grips my wrist. He spins me around, his other arm coming around my neck, squeezing. He's got me in a chokehold, but I don't fight him. I can't.

"Close your eyes," he coos in my ear, his voice dropping low. "Think about how you feel when you fight. That ache that nudges you, a hunger that tightens low in your belly. You've always felt it. All your life, it's been there. Think about it, Eliana." His words are gentle murmurs in my ear, raspy and gravelly.

"Yes," I whisper, my body trembling.

"Now think about your sister. Recall her long dark hair, her eyes that used to shine with amusement. Her soft giggle. You're both fourteen," he tells me as if he's there, watching us. "You're lying on the grass in the sunshine. She's reading a book."

"I . . . I'm telling her something."

He nods beside me. I feel the movement against my face. The roughness of his stubble scratching me, causing goosebumps to dot my skin.

"Meredith, I don't know what to do. It hurts so much." My voice is an imploring whisper. My body has been changing

for months. My breasts are bigger than hers, and there's an ache low in my stomach. I don't know how to stop it, to make it go away.

"Go to the doctor, Eliana. You're sick. You need help," she sneers. It's the first time I've ever seen her like this.

"Are you angry with me?" I feel like an admonished child. We're only fourteen, and since we've been spending time with Asher and Darick, she's been different. Yes, we're still close, but her game of hide and seek has gotten out of hand.

"You should stay in your own room tonight. I'm tired of being your crutch," she sighs, not answering my question. My heart aches. She's my twin, my other half, but lately she's felt so far away, and I don't know how to fix this between us. My phone buzzes, and I notice it's Darick. "Who's that?" Her question startles me. Dropping the phone on her blanket, she grabs for it, and I'm not fast enough. When her eyes fall to the name on the screen, she meets my gaze with fury. "Why do you have to take everything that's mine!"

Her screech is volatile, echoing around the garden, making my ears hurt.

"Girls! What's going on out here?" Daddy steps out with lemonade and sandwiches, crowding around us, possibly to

stop the fight about to ensue.

"Nothing. She keeps taking my things. Leave me the hell alone," Meredith whispers in a dangerous tone. She slams the phone against my chest, knocking the breath from my lungs.

"That's enough, Meredith!" our father roars. "Eliana, just leave. I'll come see you shortly," he orders me, and I obey with tears stinging my eyes. I don't understand. Why does she hate me so much?

"What did you remember, Eliana?" Asher's voice drags me back to the present where his arms are still wrapped around me. When I confided in my sister, about Asher and me, wanting him to kiss me and touch me, she told me I was stupid. But it was Darick's message on my phone that broke something between us.

"Meredith and Darick," I manage to mumble.

He spins me around, his hands cupping my face. "Tell me." It's an order, and I try to nod.

"I wanted my sister to care. She thought I was fucked up because I wanted . . ."

"Me? Darick?" He finishes my sentence, and I nod, and I realize how much my sister and I were at odds,

even then. His face falls into a serious expression. "What happened?"

"That day I got a message from your brother. She saw Darick's name on my phone and went crazy. She told me to stop stealing everything that's hers." My words are scratchy, clawing at my throat with emotion that threatens to choke me. "Asher, did I . . . I mean . . . you said I was yours?"

"You were, Eliana. You still are," he confirms with a nod.

"But why would she say that? And why would Darick be messaging me?" My questions fall between us, hanging in the air, and the possibility of what it means only seems to darken Asher's eyes even more. There's unbridled rage simmering in the dark orbs as he pins me with a stare.

"There are things we did. We played a game, Eliana." He turns, stalking through to the kitchen. When he returns, he's holding a glass of water, the ice clinking against the sides.

I reach for it, thankful for the refreshing drink. Once I've gulped down half, I meet his gaze. "What game

did we play? I need to know," I implore him, my tone frustrated. "What happened to me, Asher?"

He drops his hands at my question, and he doesn't respond. Instead, he steps back and sighs loudly. The tightness in his shoulders, the tension in his back are signs he's at war with himself. I want to reach out and touch him, but I don't.

"We played truth or dare. We . . ." He turns his stare from me to the window, watching the city flit by. "The three of us were close, too close sometimes." He falls silent, considering what to tell me. At least, that's what I think he's doing. All I want is the truth.

For years, I've been living in the dark, and now that he's here, telling me there's more to my past, I can't ignore that. Whenever I tried remembering my sister or the night she died, I never could pinpoint what happened. All these years I've put it down to the trauma, but there must be more to it.

There has to be so much more, and I intend to find out what.

"How close?"

He spins on his heel to face me again. Eyes blazing

with fury. "Darick wanted you as much as I needed you. There were nights when I was in your room when we'd do things I shouldn't have been doing." His body vibrates with rage and fear. A lethal combination that's surely about to rip me apart, and I realize I want it. He reaches for my hair, gripping it fiercely in his fist. "Get on your fucking knees," he growls, and I can't stop my descent because his hold is too strong. He forces me down. Once I'm kneeling, he leans in, his face close to mine. "You will stay here, not moving until I come back. Do you understand me?"

I try to nod, but I can't move. "Yes, Asher," I murmur, and the anger dissipates as fast as it appeared. He releases the hold he has on me, turns, and stalks away, leaving me trembling, needy, and filled with confusion.

A soft buzzing sounds and I notice the blinds closing over the large windows that overlook the city. Once they're shut, it's dark. I can't see my hand in front of my face, and I wonder what he's doing. It's silent. My hearing pricks trying to make out a sound, anything, but there's nothing.

My knees hurt from the cold tiles. I want to move,

but I don't. Moments pass, minutes, hours, I don't know, but I'm exhausted from the long flight. The ache between my legs from Asher fucking me is still present, and my scalp tingles from his harsh treatment.

"This was meant to be done differently, but you're pushing me, Eliana," he tells me from the darkness, startling me. I can't see him, but I can tell he's nowhere near me. "That night was when everything changed. We loved each other so much. Darick, you, and me." I frown at the words. That doesn't make sense. Meredith and Darick were together. At least, that's what it seemed like in the memories that have flashed through my mind.

Asher still doesn't turn on a light, and I don't hear him moving. Instead, I'm left alone in the darkness with my mind whirling with possibilities.

"I wanted so much to take you, to share you with Darick. We were close once—my brother and me. I can't tell you what happened, Eliana. You'll need to remember on your own, but to my brother, you were perfect. He reveled in your innocence, and I basked in your corruption. But I wasn't the one to turn you onto that darkness; it was him. Darick always knew how to

manipulate."

"I still don't understand," I rasp.

"Truth or dare, Eliana?" he asks from my left somewhere.

"Dare."

"Close your eyes. You're in your bedroom. I'm beside you, and the window is open. You're fifteen. It's about a week before your sixteenth birthday." Once again, he tells me a story. He is there, in a memory, while I'm attempting to picture it.

"Okay."

"My hands are on you, under your pale blue dress, the one with big flowers on it." I gasp at the image that immediately flits in my mind. It's real. A memory. I shut my eyes so tight in an attempt to hold onto it. "You tell me—"

"I want you to feel me. I want to be yours. Please touch me, Asher," I beg. The same words from that night. I recall taking his hand, placing it on my small breast. I was tiny at fifteen. He was far older, more experienced. I wanted him to see me as a woman.

"When you're old enough, I'll take you, Eliana," he tells

me from within the room, but also within my memory. His lips move closer as he plants a kiss on my forehead. It's strangely gentle, but his hand mauls my teenage tit.

"Why not now?" I whine. I sound like a child. Like my sister would.

"Eliana is just a slut," Meredith's voice comes through, taunting me. We both leap from my bed to see her standing in the adjoining bathroom glaring at us.

"Leave us alone!" I screech. Knowing Daddy isn't home, she chuckles.

"Soon you'll find out what it's like, little sister. Then you'll not be so eager to beg men to break your virginity." Her words sound ominous. As if she knows. It only angers me more. I'm almost sixteen, and I can't believe I have to wait another year.

When I glance up, my sister is gone, and in her place is Darick. His hand is on his crotch, watching. "Why is Darick here?" I question to the darkness, to the man beside me in my mind.

"You know he loves you. He likes to see you enjoy yourself," Asher coos in my ear. I shudder and nod. I do know, and I love how he watches me.

He falls silent, then a single light comes on, illuminating his face. Shadows dance along his jaw, making him look like an avenging angel.

My eyes snap open, and I'm breathing hard, ragged. My lungs feel too tight. "From what you're saying, I was a teenage whore for you and Darick?" I bite out frustrated.

He chuckles darkly. "Oh no, darling, you were no whore. You lost your innocence to that asshole." He spits the last word as he mentions Michael. "You remember your sister's words?" He asks, and I nod. "Good, because when you learn about what happened, you need to keep in mind she wasn't herself."

"Wasn't herself?" I question as he nears me. Offering me a hand, he helps me to stand.

"Once you recall the last moments of your sister's life, it will all come crashing back."

"What if I can't? If nothing comes back to me?"

"You're already remembering. You just need to open yourself to it," he assures me, leading me to the sofa. He heads over to turn on the downlights in the ceiling.

"Tell me more," I implore him, slipping my hand

into his when he takes a seat beside me.

He pulls me up until my body is flush with his. “We spent every summer together, in the forest. Those warm evenings on the pool deck where we’d play truth or dare,” he smirks. Tipping his head to the side, he allows his gaze to dance across my face. “You loved hearing about our lives.” His words cause me to tremble in his arms. “You knew one day you’d be one of us.”

“Can we go on a job?”

He shakes his head. “We can train in the gym.”

“I’d like that,” I inform him.

“Aren’t you tired, vixen?” He leans in, kissing my neck, suckling the flesh into his mouth.

“Let’s fight.” Two words and he chuckles.

Meeting my gaze, he suddenly seems too serious, and my heart squeezes. “Michael would be happy to take you as his wife so he can claim your father’s fortune,” he grunts, releasing my face.

“And you wouldn’t?” I quip.

“I don’t need your father’s empire. I have my own. But, if we did end up married, joining the two would allow us to rule the fucking world.”

"So, you want me because you want to—"

"I want you, Eliana," he bites out, interrupting my tirade. "Because I've wanted to fucking claim you since I was seventeen. Do not confuse my business wants with my desires. Even if you were a nobody, I'd want you."

Folding my arms in front of my chest, I regard him through narrowed eyes. "Why? Why do you want me so much?"

"Because your darkness plays well with mine. The fantasies you touch your pretty cunt to are the things I crave to do to you. All these years, you're the only woman who has calmed the filthy beast inside me that loves to fuck hard and dirty, that hungers to kill and drench itself in blood. And more than that, you're the only woman who's made me love." He sets me on the sofa and stalks away, leaving me gaping at his honesty.

ASHER

I reach the gym with my body still shuddering. Pulling off my shirt, I drop it on the floor. I know she'll follow. Her curiosity was always what brought her to me. She would find me when I tried my hardest to hide.

The sky flickers with pinpricks of yellow lights from every home in the city view. The tension has my muscles tight in my shoulders. Raking my hand through my hair, I inhale a deep breath.

"You want a fight?" Her tentative whisper comes from behind me, but I don't turn. I can't look at her with the rage racing through me. The words that taper off leave me wanting to finish her sentence. To give her the answer, but I refrain. Holding on to the last bit of my self-resistance, I watch the busy city below.

"Eliana, you don't know what you're asking of me. I fight to kill. You're tired. We need to rest before you can

even attempt taking me down." It's true.

"Fuck you, Asher. I'm not some broken little girl you can keep locked in a tower anymore. Show me. Turn around and face me." Her words squeeze my lungs, causing me to spin around. My hand quickly grips her throat.

"This what you wanted?"

"Truth or dare, Asher?" she gasps, clawing at my hand which is now lifting her onto her tiptoes. She won't be able to fight me. She'll never be able to take me down. "Fucking answer me." Her voice is raspy, but she still has a fire blazing in her eyes.

I drop her to the ground. "Dare."

"Fight me." Her jade eyes peek up at me from under those fair lashes. She's on the floor, on her knees. I'm about to respond when she moves swiftly, grabbing my ankle and tugging me down alongside her.

My legs swing out, attempting to grip her between my thighs, but she's too quick, like a gazelle. Once she's grounded, her stance widens, ready for my attack. We round each other warily, eyes glued to our opponent.

She runs toward me suddenly, her small fist making

contact with my abdomen, knocking the breath from me momentarily. I take the opportunity to grip her wrists, my foot knocking her off balance as I land on top of her, pinning her to the mat.

"Truth or dare, Eliana?" I ask, inhaling deep breaths.

"Truth."

"Close your eyes and tell me about the night you met me," I whisper, our chests heaving as she flips us over. She's straddling me, holding onto me. Her eyes flutter closed, her brows furrow in concentration.

Silence surrounds us. Frustration ebbs from Eliana. It must be difficult not to remember anything, to lose so much of what you once held dear. "I can't," she whispers almost painfully.

"Listen to me, hear my voice. The first words I said to you were, 'You're a white-haired princess who needs an adventure,' while you leaned over the balcony of the dining room of Calloway mansion."

She gasps in surprise, then tells me about that night. "It was a dinner party. Black tie. You were wearing a black shirt and white tie. You told me you hated conforming. You and Darick were dressed identically."

"Good girl." I flip her over once more, her body soft and pliable beneath mine. "Tell me about the first time I kissed you."

She's silent for so long I'm certain I've lost her, but then another inhale from her lips tells me something's just unlocked in her mind. Her eyes hold affection. "I loved you." The confession stills us both.

I lean in, my mouth inches from hers. "Loved?" I question in anticipation. Our eyes flit back and forth, left and right. I hold my breath in the hope that this memory being unlocked will not have her walking out on me.

"Love. I still love you." She blinks as she admits it, the tears she's been holding back flow freely, and I lap them up, tasting her emotion, reveling in the salt trickling on her cheeks.

I don't know how effective the hypnotherapy will be. Not with what she's suppressing. I learned a long while ago that Eliana has Dissociative Amnesia from that night, mainly due to the trauma she witnessed. I wish I could forget that night.

"You need to rest. Tomorrow we start the first part of your hypnotherapy, and I want you alert," I say, moving

off. Once she's standing beside me, I meet her gaze. "I love you." She blushes at my words, nods, then laces her fingers in mine.

In the bathroom, I let her shower alone. We've fucked twice. I've been inside her, claimed her. But I know she'll need space to allow her mind to catch up to all the emotions she's feeling.

We both brush our teeth, watching each other in the mirror. Our reflections show a normal couple, something we never were. When we reach my bedroom, I allow her to choose the side of the bed she likes and watch her curl up under the sheet. I head back to the shower and allow the spray to calm my muscles. Once done, I pull on a pair of sweats and slip under the covers beside her. In her sleep, she rolls over, draping herself over me. Her soft, shallow breaths calm me.

The room is dark now. I can't see much, but I don't need to. I feel her heartbeat against my chest and her soft breaths in my neck. She's fallen asleep. All the tension, excitement, and truths have finally worn her out.

"What are you doing here?" I ask in a hushed tone in the darkness, knowing he's there, watching. That's

always been like Darick, the voyeur.

"Needed to see you finally claim her," he tells me from the shadows. He's silent, but I feel him move to the bedside. "She's yours. I'll help you with her. I respect your choice." I know it hurts him to tell me that. But he knew, even then, Eliana would always be mine. There was no question.

"She'll do it, Darick. You don't need to be here."

"I'm here to see Oliver and Dillon for a job. I did enjoy the show though. It was utterly delicious," he says, and I can hear the smirk in his tone.

"Goodbye, brother." I close my eyes, knowing he'll be gone in moments. My arm is crossed over my eyes, the other one draped around my girl, and that's how I fall asleep.

A noise startles me awake, and I turn over to find Eliana gone. My heart leaps into my throat, choking me with the intensity of its thudding. Shoving off the sheet I'm tangled in, I head into the living room.

I breathe a sigh of relief when I see her seated,

crossed-legged on the carpet, watching the dark sky. I'm not sure what the time is, but it's probably close to dawn. I make my way closer to her, noticing she's dressed in my shirt and nothing else. The sight is incredible.

"I couldn't sleep," she tells me, not turning to face me. "Who were you talking to?" Her question jars me for a moment before I settle beside her. I don't respond, keeping my eyes trained on the window, and even though I can't see her reflection, I know her brows are furrowed in confusion.

"Darick," I tell her.

"He was here?" She turns her head toward me. I can almost hear the questions screaming in her head. Knowing he was here only makes things more complicated. "Why was he in the bedroom?"

"I thought you were asleep," I respond, not answering her question.

"What was he doing in the bedroom?" she asks again. "Asher, I need to know."

Sighing, I turn to her, hoping this isn't going to undo everything I've worked on with her over the time we've found each other again. "He was watching us," I

explain through clenched teeth. I bite down so hard, my jaw hurts.

She gasps in surprise, her eyes swimming with even more questions. "Why?"

"He's a voyeur. He gets off watching. It's his thing," I answer, telling her more about Darick than I care to. He's always loved watching. It's how he's been since he was a teenager. The first time I caught him in my bedroom, I was sixteen. He watched me fuck a girl while he jerked himself to orgasm, and I let him. I allowed him into my personal space, and she didn't know.

"And he enjoys watching us?" I nod at her question. "I see." She turns back to the window, and I can't see her expression in the dark. "I like being here. Your place has a feeling of calm."

"You're not angry." It's not a question; it's a statement, shock filling my voice.

"Why would I be? I know now who is taunting me. If your brother enjoys watching, then it's him that's been calling me."

"What?" Snapping my gaze on her, I frown in confusion. "What are you talking about?"

"I thought it was you. In my room at the mansion, I saw you talking to someone. The man was shrouded in darkness, and I couldn't tell who it was. But that night I got a call," she murmurs, dropping her head almost in shame. "He made me touch myself. A camera in the room gave him access to see what I was doing. I wanted it." She turns to me then, pleading with her eyes for me to understand. "I wanted him to see me come apart, but he didn't allow it. Instead, he ordered me to bed after a few minutes. I've only ever spoken to him once after that. On the flight."

"This doesn't make sense. Darick wouldn't have done something like that. He likes being in the same room." I shake my head. It doesn't sound like my brother. He wouldn't fuck with Eliana like that. If he wanted her, he had every right to lay claim on her.

"It has to have been him. He told me . . ." Her words taper off into the silence.

"What did he tell you?"

"He said I need to break you. To ensure you fall. His voice was filled with rage." She sounds sad as she voices the words.

"My brother and I haven't always seen eye to eye, but this doesn't sound like him. You've heard him speaking in the car. Did you recognize his voice?"

She shakes her head. "That's not his voice, but he may have changed it on the call. There was a sort of robotic sound to it. As if he had a voice emulator."

Something doesn't feel right. Not at all. I scroll to my last dialed contacts and hit call on Dillon's number. I know for a fact he'd be awake already, and when he answers, he sounds like he's not been to sleep.

"What can I do for you, mate?"

My eyes are on her, locked on the beautiful woman who's been my world for all this time. But my mind is everywhere all at once. The need to find out who the fuck is messing with her has me playing out scenarios in my mind. "I need a trace on a call made to Eliana's phone—"

"There's no number," she whispers as she rises to full height.

"Anything for a mate of Oliver's," Dillon answers over the line.

"See you at seven. It's way too early right now." I

hang up before he has time to respond. Pulling her into me, I wrap my arms around her small frame. "He'll find out who it is." It's a promise. If there's one thing I'm sure of, it's that Dillon's connections can locate this asshole.

ELIANA

The stranger pins me down, his hand gripping my throat with enough pressure to cause tears to form in my eyes and me to reach up and claw at his hand. It's not enough though. He's too strong. His eyes blaze with fury, anger trickling from his pores as he sneers above me.

My body is flush against his. All the hard planes of his chest and torso press my soft curves to the bed. He's older, different somehow. Even in the dark, I can see it's not the man I thought it was.

"Who are you?" I choke out through sobs that seem to lodge themselves in my throat.

He doesn't respond. Instead, he chuckles darkly, causing my stomach to clench in fear. My fingers rip at his flesh, but he doesn't release me. When he leans in, his mouth comes to my ear. The hot breath that tumbles from his lips feathers over my flesh, igniting me from the inside out.

"Do you know how hard you make me when you wriggle, Poppet?" The hungry tone of his voice tickles my sensitive skin. Confusion settles on me as I try to kick my legs out, but the way he's holding me down doesn't allow me to move an inch. "Fight me, Eliana. Or try to," he taunts in a low, gravelly tone. "Because as much as you push me away, the harder I'm going to fuck you." His veiled threat sends terror skating through me. It trickles down my spine, causing my chest to burn as my lungs struggle to take in breaths.

His tongue darts out, tracing a wet, hot trail down my cheek. His teeth graze my flesh as he bites down, suckling on the skin that's tingling with an awareness that this could be my end. I'll die here, on my bed in the dark. And nobody can stop it.

"No! Please!"

"Eliana." A deep rumble comes from beside me, shuddering through me, causing me to jolt upright in bed. My body is shaking. Tears streak down my face, and I turn to find familiar brown eyes staring at me in shock. "Are you okay, baby? What was that?"

Asher has his hands on my shoulders, holding me

steady because it feels as if I'm about to topple over. I can't do this. Shoving him off me, I dart out of bed and rush to the bathroom. As soon as I'm at the toilet, I double over, and the burning bile that's been rising in my throat exits my mouth in a violent retch.

Hands hold my hair. His soft, calming voice comes from behind me, and his other hand strokes my back gently. Tears prick my eyes, readying themselves to fall once more. My body convulses angrily at the memory, the dream, whatever that was as I throw up nothing. It burns. Stings. I'm shaking by the time it stops and then cocooned in warm, strong arms. My body feels small and frail.

"Baby," Asher murmurs into my hair, planting a kiss on the crown of my head. My head feels heavy, filled with unwanted thoughts and images. I can't shake the nightmare. There's nothing that can stop it because every time I close my eyes, those wretched eyes are glaring down at me.

"Tell me what happened the night my sister died," I ask him in the silence of his immaculate bathroom. He's quiet, not responding to me while he gently strokes my

back. I'm not sure I want to know, but I need to. The truth needs to come out. I need to know why I've blocked it out.

Something terrible must have happened. Something so horrific that my mind has decided it's best for me to forget.

"Not here. Not now, Eliana."

"Why am I broken?" I ask, my voice small and confused. Lifting my gaze to meet the browns of Asher's, I implore him to tell me, to give me something.

"Dillon said he's ready. Three sessions will hopefully break your mental block. We can start with the treatment today. We'll take you through hypnosis, and that will allow you to remember."

"Will it really work?" I sound hopeful. Needing to know what happened, and knowing that no matter what, Asher will be there sets me at ease even if it is only for a short time.

"We hope so." He lifts me, scooping me in his arms bridal-style, and sets me on the counter. He fills a glass with water, offering it to me to rinse my mouth. His eyes are on me all the time, watching, almost as if he's

waiting for me to do something. "Will you tell me about the dream?"

Sighing, I spit the water into the basin and meet his enquiring gaze. "A man was trying to choke me. He called me Poppet, like the caller on the phone."

Asher's eyes simmer with rage, his body is still, but it's his eyes that seem to come alive. They dance and flicker like a flame. Danger oozes from every pore of this man's body, but the fire that rages in those mocha orbs is enough to snuff out any enemy.

"We'll find him. I swear to you, and when we do . . ." His jaw ticks; his words are gritted out through clenched, white teeth. His hands fist and release and I half expect him to detonate just from the anger that seems to simmer inside him. Like a tea kettle, he is nearing boiling point, and I fear when he finally explodes, there'll be nothing but destruction in his wake.

"I believe you. I do." I reach for his hand, hoping to calm him for a moment.

Suddenly, he's lifting me off the counter, walking me into the bedroom, and setting me on the bed. He doesn't speak as he moves about the room, pulling on

his jeans and a black T-shirt that hugs his lean, muscled frame. He pulls out a pair of sweatpants from a drawer and a small pink tank top, both my size.

"Put these on. We're leaving," he orders, stalking from the room.

Confusion settles in my gut as I pull on the clothes, wondering how he had exactly my size. Once I'm dressed, I slip my feet into the ballet pumps I was wearing on the flight and hasten into his living room. He's on the phone, but his eyes spark when they land on me.

"We need to do this now. She needs to remember. I want it done in one session, not three." He hangs up and saunters toward me. "Dillon will be ready for us when we get to his place. Tonight, you'll know everything. The truth." His words are ominous, and my stomach tumbles with anxiety.

"Asher, promise me you won't leave me?" I'm not sure why I'm so fearful he's about to walk away from me. But the dread that surfaces is claustrophobic.

"I'll never leave you." It's a vow. I nod, and we head toward the exit. No more words are spoken as we make our way to the parking lot. We reach a black BMW X5

SUV that sits in a spot in the far corner, and Asher opens the passenger door for me. Once I've slipped into the seat, he shuts me in and makes his way to the driver's side.

Even though he's not speaking, I feel his words around me. Holding me, keeping me safe. As if he's emanating everything, he's trying to tell me with his actions. The engine purrs to life, and his hand finds my thigh as he drives out onto the road. It's strange being on the wrong side of the street as the traffic moves through the city.

"I'm scared," I tell him honestly.

"I know. So am I. But we need to do this. You need to know what happened, and the reason you can't remember is that the trauma of that night has forced your mind to forget, and the drugs they plied you with, that didn't help. It only suppressed the memories even more."

"How am I going to remember then?" I glance at him. His hand on the steering wheel is tight. White knuckles grip the black leather so hard I'm sure he would be able to crush it into pieces.

"Dillon will hypnotize you. He'll take you back to that night," he tells me without even glancing my way. The hand he has on my thigh tightens reassuringly, then releases. "I need you to promise me one thing, Eliana."

"Anything," I tell him, my eyes burning a hole into the side of his face.

"Whatever you remember, don't hate me for walking away. Give me time to explain why I did it. And then you can decide." The ominous feeling returns full force as his words sink in.

"Did you want to walk away?" This time, he glances at me. My question is raw, scraping at my throat.

"No," he says on a swallow. His voice husky, pained. "I never wanted to leave you. But I had no choice. Because of my father, I was made to leave. If only I had been strong enough to fight . . ." His words taper off as he weaves through the traffic.

I have no idea what he means, but deep down, I know if he had a choice, he would've stayed. He's told me he loved me, still loves me, so there must have been something that would've hurt him and me that made him leave.

Moments later, we're pulling up to a gate which guards a house on the outskirts of the city. The building behind the ornate black trellis looks like a castle. Silently, the car makes its way closer, and we stop right outside the front door.

The driveway has two similar-looking cars parked not far from where we stopped, and Asher groans beside me.

"What?" I question, glancing at him.

"My brother is here as well," he says before exiting the car and rounding the front. Opening my door, he helps me out on shaky legs. Before we reach the oak door, it slides open, and I'm met with the dark eyes of Dillon.

"Darling," he smirks while reaching for my hand. He lifts it to his lips, pressing a kiss on my knuckles. "How are you this morning?"

"Fine, thank you," I smile, noticing the hunger in his gaze.

Asher leans in, whispering in my ear, "if you're thinking of having him and my brother watch us, I'd gladly assist."

An ache stretches itself out like a cat in my belly, clawing at my stomach, tingling down to my pussy. I want him to watch me again. Dragging a gaze to Asher, he grins; it's knowing. This man knows everything about me, better than I know myself.

"You're thinking something naughty, doll face?" he taunts, leaning into me, his lips against my ear. The heat of his breath sending a shiver through me.

"Perhaps," I respond. Dillon shakes his head, but the wicked smile on his mouth is a clear indication he knows what is going on. He turns and leads us farther into the cavernous house. It's old, with nineteenth-century architecture and the furnishings remind me that this is an old-style English manor.

The maze of hallways we follow takes us deep into the bowels of the house.

"Is Darick here?" Asher questions from beside me.

"Yeah, he arrived late last night, or early this morning. I can't remember," Dillon informs us as he pushes open a dark, cherry wood door. As soon as I step inside, I can't help gasping. It's like a dungeon, but it's decadent. The reds and browns give it a warm feeling,

but in the corner is a cage, a prison cell. There are no windows, which makes it gloomy apart from the yellow lightbulbs.

A desk filled with computer equipment sits to the left, opposite the cage.

"Welcome to my humble abode," Dillon says, offering me a seat. The chair is wingback, intricately chiseled to a delicate pattern of vines and leaves. The velvet a Merlot color which matches the room perfectly. It screams money, class, and opulence.

"I'd hardly call it humble," I tell him as the door behind us swings open and I'm met with brown eyes the same color as Asher's. My gaze darts between the two brothers, and I realize the only difference between them are their hair color. Where Asher is raven-haired, Darick is white-blonde, almost matching my own.

"The lovely Eliana Calloway," he says, stepping closer to me. I rise, immediately needing to stand in the presence of the three men. He gives me a small nod, then turns his gaze on Asher. "Brother, good to see you again."

"You're staying?" Asher questions.

The air crackles between them, and I wonder if a fight will ensue.

"Simmer down, boys," Dillon chuckles. "There's no pissing contest here, and if you both really want to whip out your cocks, I'm sure Eliana and I will be happy to compare sizing."

Both brother's pin him with a glare at his joke, but I can't help giggling to myself. Darick's eyes meet mine, and there's a tiny flicker of recognition in my mind of him. But as soon as it appears, it's gone in the next second.

"Don't be an asshole, Dillon," Asher smirks.

ASHER

"Can we just have one day where the two of you can get along?" my best friend questions as he sits at the desk. He starts tapping on the keyboard, and I settle myself on the chair opposite his desk, which is messy with papers and old food containers.

I pull Eliana onto my lap, making her squeal as she flops her pert little ass on my thighs.

"Also, keep it clean. We have work to do," Dillon chastises me like a fucking child. I pin him with a glare as I roam my hands over Eliana's thighs. I notice how his eyes wander over her body following the trail of my hands.

Eliana shivers as I reach her stomach, my one hand moving up, the other moving south.

"Asher, please." Her plea is enough to spur me on. She's always been a little nymph. Since I knew her, she's

taunted me, teased me, loving every second of how much I wanted her. Now that I have her, I'm going to show her just how much pleasure there is in life. I will give her what she needs.

Her head drops back when my fingers stroke her mound through the sweatpants she's wearing. Her heat is evident, and I wonder just how wet she is right now.

"Do you like that, vixen? Both of them watching us," I murmur in her ear. She nods her head, her lips parting on a soft moan that has me growing hard. We should be working, fixing her, but right now all I can think of is being inside her, feeling her again and again. Having both Dillon and Darick watch as I claim my girl turns my body molten. Their gazes burn through us, and they're close to losing control, while I continue my ministrations, causing her to whimper loudly. Her grip on the arms of the chair tightens. She's practically clawing at the material.

Lust hangs heavy in the air with the four of us beyond turned on. In the dark, where all our demons come to play, we revel in the sinful acts. Eliana whimpers when her ass presses against my erection. A groan falls from

my lips when I lift my hand to her mouth, my middle finger trapped between her plump lips as she sucks on it. Darick stalks closer, settling himself on the edge of the desk, his eyes glued to our movements. I pull my finger from her mouth and dip it under the waistband of her clothes, realizing when I feel the wetness that she doesn't have any panties on underneath, then finding her throbbing clit.

Dillon joins us then. He leans in, pressing a soft kiss to my girl's plump lips. "Do you like him kissing you, vixen?" I question using her nickname because right now, all I want is her to feel good. To calm down. Her body writhes above me. Dillon reaches for her nipples, tweaking them through the material of her tank top.

"Dillon, Asher," she moans our names, calling us to take what we need and in turn, give her what she wants, what she hungers for.

Darick moves closer. His hands on her face, cupping her cheeks, he kisses her lips, tentatively, but he doesn't allow his tongue to delve into her mouth. I shove off her sweatpants. She's open now, bare to the two men I trust with my life, and I wouldn't have it any other way.

Yes, she's mine, I've claimed her, but only when I give permission will she have another man touch her.

"Did you want to get toyed with by all three of us?" I hiss in her ear, causing her to shudder. Dillon moves behind Darick, lifting the tee my brother is wearing off while I spread Eliana's legs wide with my own, hanging them over my thighs. She's open, inviting, and Darick doesn't waste time crashing his mouth on her wet, hot cunt. Her cries are loud, bouncing off the walls. Eliana moans softly as Darick devours her with hunger. His tongue's dancing along her clit, dipping into her heat.

Once he rises, his mouth is glistening with her juices. Then Dillon's hands are on my cock, pulling me out of my pants, stroking me with animalistic desire. His fist is vise-like as he moves up and down, making me groan. It's not the first time we've done this, shared a woman, but it's the only time I've been in love with her. I can't stop my hips from bucking toward his fist. His eyes burn with desire.

My body is wound tight. Seeing them worship her, taunt her, it sets me in motion. My best friend releases my shaft, and I slip into her hole, easily dipping in deep.

Dillon takes position between her thighs, his mouth latching onto her as I plunge into her body. His tongue laps at her at where we're joined.

Darick slides Dillon's jeans down, and I watch his saliva drip onto the puckered hole of my best friend. I've seen them fuck once before, but this is something else entirely. He works his fingers into Dillon, finger-fucking him, loosening him up for a thick, hard cock. Soon, Dillon is moaning against Eliana, and she's whimpering, practically bouncing on my cock.

Everything about this moment is filthy, it's sinful, and I can't stop. I don't want to.

"Asher, oh God," Eliana moans.

"Watch them, baby," I order her, causing her to glance up at Darick and Dillon.

My mind is gone. My hands are on Eliana's breasts, tweaking and tugging her nipples. I know her eyes are glued to Darick as his body — toned, filled with ink — moves behind the man eating her pussy like it's his last meal. Dillon moans loudly against Eliana and me when Darick sinks into his ass.

The sounds of fucking — pure, raw, and filthy —

echo like a song. Skin slapping. Wet juices of my woman's cunt cause my balls to draw up. I breathe through it, not wanting to let go. But I know I won't last long. The four of us move in tandem.

Back and forth.

In and out.

Faster. Harder. Deeper.

I can't breathe when my eyes roll back and pleasure rockets through every inch of my body. My nerves are electric; the blood rushing through my veins is on fire. I'm burning with hunger. Dillon's mouth is on my balls. He sucks them hard into his mouth as my cock gets buried inside Eliana's tight pussy.

"Asher," she cries, screams my name.

There's a grunt from Darick, and a low growl from Dillon and I know they've just found their release. With a moan, and then I'm lost in the euphoria of Eliana's orgasm as she pulses around me and I fill her with my seed once more. I don't know how long I sit there motionless. I don't recall the moment she moves, but when I open my eyes, she's kneeling between my thighs, lapping at my wet dick.

"Jesus," Darick murmurs as he tucks himself back into his jeans. Dillon is also righting himself, but his eyes are glued to my girl, my fucking woman who is a siren if ever I saw one. And I wonder if she's going to lure me to my death, or if her love for me will save us both.

I lift her in my arms, her body floppy and her eyes sleepy as I carry her from the office down the hall toward one of the many bedrooms of the mansion. I set her on the bed gently, and her gaze meets mine.

"I'm sorry," she mumbles, her lashes fluttering against her pink cheeks.

Allowing my fingers to stroke her face, I frown in confusion. "What?"

"That will . . ." She points toward the door. "I wanted it so much."

I settle on the bed beside her, pulling her closer, needing to hold her.

"Asher, it's my fault she's dead. Isn't it?"

"No, it's not your fault. And I never want you to apologize for needing sex. Your body is beautiful, and although I'll never allow them to fuck you, they're welcome to taste what is mine." A small shiver races

through her at my words. "I understand that need, that deep-seated yearning." I release her, lifting her face so we're eye to eye. "I want to give you what you need, Eliana, and if it means having incredible sex like that, I'll do anything for you."

"You mean you're not angry with me for enjoying that?" I shake my head as her question is innocent, and yet so confused.

"You need to feel the high. I know how much it can rule you. But you're special, my sweet girl. You've used your training to sate it. What happened in that room was one of the best moments of my life," I tell her.

"Honestly, it was one of mine as well. Sometimes I feel like I'm so fucked up for wanting it. Needing to be watched. But then, when I'm watching someone die, it's still there. I feel it more than ever. I'm sick, Asher." Her words gut me. They break into my chest and squeeze my heart.

"You're not sick. If you believe that, then it means we're both fucked up."

"Then I guess we'll be fucked up together," she quips, causing me to grin. Shaking my head, I wrap her

in my arms and hold her close. Soon, she'll remember the night her sister died, and a new set of memories will bring guilt along with them. But it will also bring about rage, anger, and even more so, the need for vengeance.

"Rest. I'll come get you when we're ready to start. I'll give Dillon your phone to try to trace the calls. Also, I think the guys need a moment before they can focus on anything but your sweet little cunt," I tell her, pressing a kiss to her mouth. Her giggle is so carefree, and I want to listen to it forever on repeat. But we have a long way to go before we ever reach that moment.

I leave her on the bed and make my way back to the office to see if Dillon is ready to start this shit.

ELIANA

My body aches, but I feel better than I have in years. I roll over on the bed, feeling the empty space beside me, and I realize Asher must be with Dillon and Darick. A vibration on the mattress startles me — my phone. I thought Asher had given it to Dillon, perhaps he'd forgotten.

Pulling it from my pocket, I glance at the unknown number staring back at me. Swiping my finger over the screen, I press the phone to my ear before answering.

"Hello?"

"You promised me something, Poppet. I trust you'll deliver," the cold, calculated tone comes from the other end of the line. My skin prickles with fear, something I never felt before because I thought it was Asher playing games with me. Now though, I have no idea who this is.

"I know what I promised, but sometimes plans

change." My words are a low whisper. I know I can find out who he is and why he's targeting me by remaining calm.

"You mistake me for an understanding man, Poppet. That I am not, perhaps I should pay a visit to your father's estate and burn it to the ground."

"There's nothing there. It's a shell."

"And while you sit in London with Asher Briggs, I'll ensure that the last will and testament your father entrusted to you will be undone. If you don't give me what I want, you will lose everything." His warning causes my blood to turn to ice. It solidifies in my veins, and I can't stop the shiver that travels through me.

"What do you know of my father's will? Michael, if you're trying to fuck with my mind, it's not going to work," I bite out, anger returning full force when he chuckles at my retort.

"Ah, Michael, the man who has had the pleasure of tasting that delicious little cunt of yours. Tell me, Poppet, does he give you the pleasure you seek? Does he satisfy those aches you hold deep down inside your broken little head? Or are those secrets still safely stowed away?"

This isn't some stranger. This is a man who knows me. Who's learned about me on a more personal level because if it isn't Asher, then it's someone who's been watching me for far longer.

"I suppose you've done your homework, but then again, anyone with enough money and power could unlock the medical records my father stored away safely. And Asher knows about my amnesia. So, if you're trying to—"

"Don't fucking toy with me, Poppet. Break Asher. I want the boys to learn that if they want what's mine, they'll pay."

"And what would stop you from breaking me and taking me down once I've done your bidding?" I push off the bed, needing to get to Asher before he hangs up. Something in my gut tells me I need to play this game smart. There's no one to fight, no one to punch, kick, or stab. This time, I need to think. Mind games always have been my weakness, and it seems he knows exactly that.

"Run to him, Poppet. Let him heal your mind, make you remember what happened that night. How you are the reason your family is broken, shattered, no longer.

And when you recall your actions from that night, see if Asher will stand by you, because the last time, he walked away. One thing you must not forget, it's always been you."

The line goes dead, and I'm left racing through a maze of hallways only to have my mind spinning wildly in a reel of fear, hesitation, and anxiety.

"Eliana." The baritone of Darick comes from behind me, causing me to spin on my heel and slam into his solid chest. His hair is white in this dim light, his eyes so dark, they shimmer like an onyx stone. He regards me with a cocky smirk, leaning on the doorjamb beside him.

"Darick, I got lost."

"You've been lost a long while, little one." His words cause my mind to tumble with the possibility that perhaps there is a chance that *Unknown* is Darick. Yes, his voice is different, but there is always a way of masking the tone or accent in a voice.

"So, you weren't with Dillon and Asher just now?"

He shakes his head. "No, went out for a smoke. What's it to you?" he questions. Tipping his head toward the left, he turns and leaves me to follow him.

"You knew Meredith." It's not a question, but he grunts and nods his head. "Did you . . . I mean, were you two . . .?" I don't know how to voice my question because deep down, I'm not sure I want to know the answer.

"I never fucked your sister," he tells me. "It's always been you, Eliana."

His words make my eyes snap to him. *It's always been you.* They resonate in my mind, falling around like a warning alarm. It's him. It has to be.

"What makes you say that?" I question, trying to steal my voice. His gaze lands on me, causing me to school my features, to ensure he doesn't see the recognition in my expression.

"The taunting little girl that seemed to break apart everything. You're the reason for all this." He waves his hand in the air. "But then again, you always did like being watched." He winks as he caresses the last word. "It's time to remember, Eliana. And when you do, don't forget what my brother and I did for you. We lost everything so you can enjoy your life," he utters almost angrily.

He stalks forward, and as we reach the office, the door swings open, and Asher's glances between his brother and me.

"Look who I found roaming the halls," Darick says, stepping by Asher and into the room.

"I woke up, and you weren't there. I got lost and walked into him." I don't know why I'm explaining myself, nothing happened, but the look on Asher's face makes me need to give him some reason why I was alone with Darick.

"It's okay, baby," he says, stepping closer to me. Leaning in, his lips meet mine in a gentle yet hungry kiss. His tongue darts out, teasing my lips open, seeking entry, and I allow him inside me. He licks into my mouth, tasting me, devouring me with one single kiss. His hands grip my hips, holding on as he groans when he feels me mold to him. "Jesus, you'll always be my end." He smirks, lacing his fingers in mine.

Once we enter the office, the other two men glance our way. "Eliana, are you ready to get the show on the road?" Dillon smirks, rising from his chair.

"Yeah, I wanted this over and done with as soon as

possible," I tell him. My gaze flits over to Darick. His eyes pierce my armor, and I know he sees my fear deep down. As much as I try to hide it, I can't. There's no keeping anything from him. Like a predator, he is silent, but his eyes tell the story of a man who can see past any façade.

I wanted to talk to Asher before I undergo the hypnosis, but I'd rather get this done and then I can focus on the caller, *Unknown*. As convinced as I am that it's Darick, I have no proof but a few words he mumbled to me in the hallway.

Farther into the room, I notice the cage sitting in the far corner. I know that's where I'm going. Perhaps whatever I'm about to remember is going to turn this game into something violent. Something more feral than I imagined.

Asher turns to me, a look on his face I'd not seen in the time we've spent together. Wariness. Possibly fear. Stepping closer to me, he places a hand on my cheek. "Are you ready?" I nod slowly. Am I? Perhaps. I don't have a choice. "Come," Asher says. Leading me to the cage, he opens the door and gestures for me to sit in the

chair at the center of the space.

"Are you tying me up?" I question, noticing the cuffs on the arms of the plush, ornate chair.

"We have to. There's a lot you'll remember, and it's easier this way." He continues to bind me to the chair and leaves me in the cell. The door open, him standing guard, and the other two men at the computers.

"Eliana, I need you to stay as calm as possible. Asher, put these on her." Dillon hands him a headset, which he perches on my head. I can't hear a thing. Their mouths are moving, but no sounds reach my ears.

Dillon nods to Darick, who in turn meets my gaze. The corner of his mouth lifts slightly, and he gives me a smile that brightens those deep brown eyes and crinkles the skin at the corner of his eyes. The knowing in his stare and the expression on his face causes my heart to thud.

"Can you hear me, Eliana?" Dillon's gentle English accent comes through the headset; his voice is low, almost soothing. I nod. He smiles from where he's sitting, taps the keys on the computer, then music plays in my ears. It's instrumental, something I've never heard before.

"I need you to close your eyes, and I'll count back," he murmurs to me.

"Okay," I say, unsure of how loud I am since I can't hear myself.

"Ten," he says, the melody causing my mind to drift. I feel sleepy as he continues. "Nine, eight, seven," he counts slowly, and drowsiness overwhelms me. "Six, five."

My hands that were gripping the chair loosen, and I'm nothing but flesh, boneless, calm, and yet my chest is tight with anxiety. How does that even happen?

"Four, three, two." His voice gets slower as he counts down. "One."

I'm floating. It's the strangest feeling not having any control. Your body is no longer your own, but something you feel separated from.

"Eliana, we're going back to that night. Seven years ago. It was Meredith and yours sixteenth birthday, December twenty-fourth. You were getting ready and Asher and Darick hadn't arrived yet. Tell me what happened."

I try to nod, but I can't. A memory slams into me,

and it feels like I'm there. The room is dark. I remember needing to turn on my lamp on the nightstand. I'm alone in my room. Meredith has just left to get ready.

"A message beeped on my phone. I . . ." Frowning, I shake my head, unsure of what I see. It's not clear, but the screen glares at me.

"It's okay, take your time," Dillon assures me.

"I messaged you, Eliana. I told you we would be there in ten minutes." Darick's voice is strained when it comes through the line. "You responded with—"

"I'll be waiting on the balcony," I interrupt Darick, as the memory clears.

"Good girl. Breathe, Eliana." Dillon murmurs again. "You're safe here. Just keep calm, and we'll break through." The music turned up a notch. It's calming, yet somehow, it's causing my heart to catapult in my chest.

"I've turned on my bedside lamp," I say it as I see it. "My room is a mess." There are clothes all over my bed. I'm sighing as I tug on another dress, which I hate. Suddenly, I'm not remembering — I'm there.

Pulling the skirt up my legs, I zip and button it. The

denim material is softer than I expected. Of course, Meredith would want something that shows off her legs. Since we've met the brothers next door, she's been wanting to grab Darick's attention, but he's made it clear she's not what he wants. The strange thing is, he's been very attentive toward me.

Since she saw his name on my phone, Meredith's been acting strangely. Going out at night, eluding her bodyguards, and I know if Daddy finds out, he'll have a fit. He wants to keep us safe, but she's been acting out dramatically, and I don't know how to show her it's dangerous being without someone to watch over her. Something tells me she's spending time with someone, a guy. I wish I knew who so I could tell dad to stop her. One day she'll get hurt.

"Eliana, are you ready?"

I glance at my sister standing in the doorway. Her body is curvaceous in the small denim skirt and the black tank top that hugs her torso so tight it looks like she's painted the damn thing on. Her heels are easily four inches, which is something I can't do. I've always hated those torturous things.

"I am." I pull on the floppy tee that hangs loosely over my small frame.

"You're wearing that?" Her sneer is enough to cause me

to frown and second guess my choice of top. I knew she'd have something to say.

"What's wrong with it?"

"I just thought you'd want something a little sexier. You are sixteen, you know, and I'm sure Asher would want to see what he's not tapping." She giggles. "I mean, you haven't had that cherry popped yet. Have you?" Her question causes me to bite my tongue at the retort, sitting heavily, just waiting to spat at her.

"Why did my sister hate me so much?" I question to no one in particular.

"I need you to focus, Eliana." Dillon's order comes through the headset, and I attempt nodding again. "Unless you need a break?"

"No. I want to do this." I sound adamant, more confident than I really feel. The anger that ripples from my sister is palpable, as if she's here.

Sighing, I turn back to my closet and rummage through the mess I made. I've always been more of a tomboy, comfortable in my jeans and Chucks. Heels and makeup were for the popular

girls, but as soon as I hit thirteen, it was the attention of the Briggs brothers that caused every female from here to the West Coast to hate me. Well, at least it felt like it.

"I'll see you downstairs, and try not to upstage me," I hear Meredith mumble as her heels click on the wooden floor just outside my door. The sounds taper off into nothing, and I'm alone once more.

I pull out a halter-neck top, which I know she'll approve. I don't want to bring too much attention to myself, or I'll have to deal with her again.

I'm just clasping the bra when a noise from my door startles me, and I spin around expecting to find either Asher or Darick, but it's neither. It's Sean Briggs. I rip my top from the bed, covering my body to his hungry glare.

My chest hurts, it physically aches when he appears in my mind. When he leers at me, I feel dirty, filthy. My stomach rolls, bile turbulent, attempting to rise like a slow-burning flame. Acid creeps up my chest.

"I can't. I can't. No." My voice sounds otherworldly.

The hands on mine feel heavy, solid, holding me down.

"No. I can't. Don't make me."

"Eliana, calm down. Breathe." I don't know whose voice it is. I want to open my eyes, to stop this, but I'm grounded in the memory. I'm inside it. Living it, breathing it.

"Mr. Briggs." My voice sounds so small as the foreboding figure of the man who I've come to know as my father's best friend looms in the doorway. He steps inside without responding, shutting the door behind him. Fear skitters through me like a thousand ants running over my skin.

"You're a beautiful girl, Eliana. Sixteen." His words drip venom as he stalks closer. "Perhaps you can show me what my sons are so enamored with," he says in a whiskey-fueled drawl. I can smell the alcohol from where I'm standing.

"Mr. Briggs, perhaps we can meet downstairs. I'm just finishing up here," I respond, my voice trembling with fear of what's about to happen. As I move a step back, he takes one forward. I'm about to shift away from the bed when his body is over mine, and I'm pinned to my mattress. The heaviness of his drunken form is too much, and I can't fight him off. Panic rises in my chest, swirling like an impending storm.

"Feel that princess?" he coos in my ear, causing bile to rise from my chest. His body ruts against me, as his hard cock pressing against my stomach. "This is what you do to every man, even my sons," he informs me with a sinister smirk that causes my body to convulse. The burning sensation of the puke in my throat makes my eyes tear up, the salty liquid stinging.

"Please, leave. I'll forget—"

His hand presses over my mouth, and his tongue snakes out, licking my neck from my collarbone up to my ear. I feel the bite of his teeth as they graze the fleshy lobe, then he suckles it into his mouth.

I can't breathe. I can't think. My small hands push at him, but it's not enough. I'm too weak. My legs flail, but all it does is make him chuckle. My body shudders, attempting to roll us over, but I'm no match for him. He knows it, and now so do I.

"I love when you wriggle, little one. It feels so good on my cock when you do that. Your sister said you'd be perfect," he tells me. My eyes widen in horror at his words. Meredith? What does he mean? My head moves left to right, but I can't shake him. I'm helpless and alone, and there's no one who's going to save me.

When my bedroom door flies open, Meredith's voice causes me to whimper, pleading behind the wrinkled fleshy hand of Sean Briggs. But she can't hear me.

My breathing is ragged as I tug on the restraints. I want to claw her eyes out, or mine. My body is alight, burning from the inside out as I feel tears streaking down my cheeks.

"Eliana, you need to keep calm. I know this is difficult, but please, breathe." Dillon's voice is in my ears, in my head. In between the memory of my sister with Sean. What was she doing? Why was she with him?

Shaking my head, I feel hands on me, cupping my face. "Vixen, I'm right here. Listen to me. You're safe. Breathe through the memory. I've got you." Asher's words ease the ache in my chest, but the bile in my throat burns as I attempt to recall the rest.

"You're still there, in the room. What's happening, Eliana?" This time it's Darick questioning me. They all want to know. I want to know, but the cry that's wretched from me causes me to choke and splutter. Anger rears its head, and I scream as it exits through me in a rage-fueled

cry. Then I'm back in the room, pressed against the bed painfully.

"Didn't I tell you she loves it?" Meredith's words sink into my brain slowly, but they don't make sense. My sister did this to me. How? Why? Sean's free hand reaches for my skirt, shoving it up, and I feel the pinch of my underwear ripped from my body. I blink, and the tears fall. They stream from my face, and I know I'll never survive this. Meredith is sitting on the bed, watching the horrific scene play out, but all she does is smile.

It's then that suddenly Sean's body is lifted off me and something crashes loud and violent. I'm still lying on my back, in shock from what happened. Meredith screeches at Darick, then Asher. Everything moves too fast. My body shoves forward, and rage spurs me into motion. I reach out, gripping my glass bedside lamp. Pivoting to face the commotion, I'm about to slam it into Sean's head when suddenly, Meredith leaps into the space between the man who almost hurt me and myself. The lamp shatters as it hits her chest, slicing through her flesh.

Blood spurts everywhere. I'm drenched in it. That's the

moment our father enters.

"Meredith! Eliana! Oh god, what have you done?" he's mumbling, holding my fucked-up sister like she's a baby. Rocking back and forth, he continues to console her now lifeless body.

"I found the two boys trying to take advantage. I'm sorry, Vic." Sean spews lies as he regards his own sons.

"Get them out of here. I want them gone. Forever," my father hisses with rage.

"No! They didn't do it! It was Sean," I plead. I'm on the floor, blood-coated and tear-stained, but he's not listening. He doesn't want to hear the truth. "Please, Daddy, listen to me. Please?"

"Eliana, go get cleaned up. We have a party to cancel and over two hundred people downstairs." Orders are conveyed, and I have no choice. So, I move, like a zombie. I watch as Asher and Darick Briggs are torn from my life forever. And Sean. He smirks as he walks behind the two boys.

My eyes snap open, and I'm breathing hard. My throat closes with a lump so thick and unyielding; I'm gulping down gusts of air. Asher is at my feet, kneeling,

his dark eyes simmering with worry, fear, and . . . Love. My knuckles are white, my grip on the chair so tight, and the cuffs are biting into my wrists painfully. My chest burns with bile at the memories slamming into me. Asher is blurry before me as tears fill my eyes.

"Get me out of here!" My voice filled with anxiety, wretched anger. "Get the fuck off me. Get me away. Get away!" I'm screeching, but he's calm. Too fucking calm. He knew.

My heart beats wildly in my throat, choking me. I try pulling in air, but my lungs don't work. Anxiety tightens my stomach, coiling like a serpent ready to strike. Ripping me to shreds as all the horrific images come flooding back. Shaking my head, I blink, and the tears flow down my cheeks.

"Baby," Asher coos, his voice low, calming, but my heart rate is through the roof as it violently attacks me with hard thuds. My breathing becomes erratic. Wild. Panic flares through me. "Eliana."

I blink once. And again. I open my mouth to respond to him but can't find the words. Sadness grips my heart, and my throat closes with emotion choking me.

It was Sean's fault. He is the reason my sister is dead. But then the truth slams me, knocking the breath from my lungs. I killed Meredith. I'm a murderer, but she wasn't a stranger. She was my sister. My twin. I only realize I'm crying when Asher reaches for my face, cupping my cheeks in his hands. His thumbs swipe the moisture away.

"Release me! Uncuff me right now!" I order. Vehemence thrums in my blood, through my veins as it surges over every inch of me. My skin is alight with the need for violence.

He immediately tugs the headset from me, then unlocks the cuffs, massaging my bruised wrists. His fingers move in gentle circles that calm me down. The silence is deafening, but after what I've experienced, I need it. I want it. Somehow, Asher knows this and gives it to me. He drags his gaze up, those beautiful mocha eyes meeting my green ones.

"I killed her. Your father. Your fucking father." My fists land on his chest, and he takes every blow. I kick, I screech, I cry. I'm shaking, vibrating with sadness so profound I once again can't breathe. But I continue my

attack on Asher. "Fuck you, fuck you Briggs'. All of you. You did this to me."

I drop to my knees, curling into a ball of regret, guilt, and anguish. And all the time, he's there. Holding me in his warm arms until I'm a puddle of pain. Nothing but a shattered little girl.

"You know everything now," he whispers then, sadness lacing his tone. "I couldn't keep you safe. And then I walked—"

"You were there for me. If it weren't for you, I'd have been violated in the worst way. What I want to know is what my father did to make you walk away. I know he told you to leave, but what was he holding over you to make you never turn around. At least until he died."

His arms are still cocooning me, and I wonder if he's trying to keep me from breaking. I clutch him to me like he's a lifeline and I'm out to shore, needing the connection to save me from drowning in guilt.

"He knew that my *career* was less than stellar. But he had a video tape of me in the house of one of the senators. I was fucking his wife after I'd killed him."

"But my father's done worse. I know he has. Why

would—?"

"Because the senator in question was Michael's brother. If that video got into the wrong hands, I would've been put away for life, or given a death sentence. Sean struck a deal. Of course, when your father died, the deal was moot." His words skitter across my skin, and I wonder why Michael never mentioned he had a brother, even if he was dead. Granted, we weren't in a relationship, but surely, he could've told me. All this time, Michael was trying to convince me not to kill for revenge, but he wanted it.

"I'm just so confused."

"We can talk later," he tells me with a nod.

Realizing I'm exhausted, I feel my eyes flutter. "I am tired. Can you stay with me?"

"Anything you want, baby, anything."

ASHER

She's been asleep for hours, and as much as I want to keep my promise to her and stay by her side, I need to finish the job we came here to do. It's just past midnight as I head out to the office. Darick glances up when I walk in, his eyes boring into me. Questions dance in them. He's dying to know what she's said, but as of now, there's not much to tell.

"Do you have the address?" I ask Dillon who's once again tapping away at his computer. He nods, pulling the printout and handing it to me.

"He's home. Wife is away with her sister on some cruise which means . . ." He tells me, his voice trickling into nothing. I know what it means. The asshole is not alone at home.

"I'm coming with you," Darick says.

I watch him for a moment before asking, "Why?"

He doesn't respond, merely shrugs as he shoves his gun into the holster on his shoulders. I don't have time to argue with my brother, so I nod and head out the door with him hot on my heels. We slip into the SUV silently, but the tension in the air is thick between us as it always is.

"Thank you," he says finally, and I flit my gaze over to him.

"For what?" I question as I turn on the engine and pull out into the quiet streets. He doesn't respond for a long while, and I wonder what's going on in my brother's head.

"Meredith was fucking Michael," he informs me easily. The revelation almost has me losing control of the car. "For years. He fucked her before she was even legal." His words are venomous. It doesn't make sense. Why would Meredith be with a man who's almost double her age?

"How do you know?" I'm curious. My brother's never one to offer more than he should. But this time, it feels like we're about to have our first heart to heart, and I don't know what to make of it. We've not been

close for years, and for him to admit something like this is strange.

"Dillon found a video on Eliana's phone from an unknown number. It was Michael nailing some chick. At first, we thought it was Eliana, but when he cleaned it up, it was Meredith." He goes silent for a little while before continuing. "Dillon worked his magic and managed to trace the origin of the video. It was sent from the Briggs mansion."

"So, you think Michael is the man taunting Eliana?"

"We don't know, but who else would it be? He's got every reason to fuck with her. And sending her a video of him with her sister is something that he would do. You know that asshole is as demented as any of the men we kill off on a normal job."

I nod. "But that doesn't mean she was with him willingly. Granted, Meredith enjoyed the challenge, but for her to be doing shit like that?"

He doesn't respond. "There's more." Two words that still my heart for a second. "Meredith was killed by Sean and Michael. I'm certain of it."

This time, I do pull off the road. "What?" My gaze is

on him, burning into him, imploring him.

"I found a list. They're all Dad's *associates*." The word is spat. I can understand why. "One of the biggest donators to the organization was Mr. O'Connell. The same time Meredith was murdered, he transferred a chunk of money into the Briggs account."

"Surely Sean would have covered that up?" I frown at Darick because I know my father wouldn't be so careless.

"Why? He can easily explain it away. He dealt in weapons."

I'm pulling up to the house where our next mark is as my mind whirls with the new information. "Fuck, this is a shit storm. I want it done, and I want to be able to move on with my life," I tell Darick, but I don't look at him. My eyes are trained on the house. The lights are off, and I know they must be in bed.

"I know." I don't respond to Darick. Instead, I exit the car and pull out my gun. The security is non-existent as we make our way over the low wall. I can't bring myself to think of what the implications would be if Meredith is still alive.

We land with soft thuds in the garden and quickly run up to the house. Darick points up, and I notice a balcony which must lead to the master bedroom. I nod. We move in sync. As much as we don't see eye to eye, there's something exciting about working with him.

There's a soft click on the front door when my brother picks the lock, and we enter quietly. We don't bother closing it, because we'll be out soon. I follow behind him as he takes the stairs two at a time. On the landing, we turn right and head down the short hallway into a bedroom. We find two sleeping forms under the comforter.

Darick moves closer, and when I follow, I notice the face of a girl who can't be more than seventeen nestled on the pillow. That only serves to anger me even more. I watch Darick point the pistol at the forehead of the man on the other side of the bed.

We don't move. Don't breathe. I await the shot, but I watch in awe as my brother does what he does best, shooting the man. I watch the bullet take off a piece of his ear. The scream that's wretched from the asshole's mouth echoes around us. The girl leaps from the bed

straight into my arms. I'm holding her as she screeches, seeing blood all over the bed. White sheets turn crimson.

"What . . . what the fuck?" The man is holding onto his face as if it's going to save him.

"This is your goodbye, Mr. Lassiter." Shooting him in the groin, then the knee, leaving him twitching as Darick smirks. I can't help wincing at another shrill scream, and my brother pulls a knife from his thigh holster, plunging it deep into the chest of our mark.

Done and dusted.

The little girl in my arms shivers as I try to appease her, sobbing as her tiny fists grip my shirt. Lifting her in a bridal-style hold, I walk out of the house and down to the car. She'll soon be home with her parents again, and I hope her life will be better than what she's had to endure.

First stop is the hospital. On the way there, we call the police. When they arrive at the hospital for her, we'll be gone. Just phantoms in the night. The less we see of the cops, the better. That's something we don't need in our lives, them sniffing into the men who saved a little girl who'd been bought and sold.

An hour later when we reach Dillon's home, I settle back in bed with Eliana. She's not moved in the two hours I've been away. Her body is tiny, curled into a little ball as I think about what Darick told me. If it's Michael calling her, then he's trying to fuck with her mind and ensure she gives in to his demands. But what he doesn't know is that I'll gut the fucker before he ever comes close to her again.

I lie back, staring at the ceiling as I wait for her to wake up again.

ELIANA

My eyes burn when I open them to the new day. My throat still aches from the screaming I did. My body feels as if it's been put through the wringer. But as sleep drifts away, the heavy arm holding me reminds me that the man I love is here.

Rolling over, I glance into a dark stare that is watching me intently.

"You're beautiful when you sleep." His words make me smile. After all the sadness I've experienced, I know I need to work my way toward a future. One with both Briggs brothers and Dillon beside me. But before we can fathom a future, we need to exact our revenge.

"Will you tell me who killed my father now?" I asked, scooting up to sit against the headboard, which is a soft velvet, pincushion style. My head hurts, the throb right behind my eyes, and I know it's because I haven't

had a proper night's rest. But every time I close my eyes, I feel him on me, over me. I still haven't told Asher about the phone call. I've also not mentioned that I think it's Darick messing with me. I was so sure it wasn't, then he uttered the exact words my *unknown* had said to me.

He scoots over, so he's sitting on the bed beside me. He looks as if he hasn't slept all night; he looks exhausted.

"Michael." One word that sends my world reeling. I'm on my knees in seconds, kneeling beside him, imploring him to tell me more with just a gentle look. The tears that pool in my eyes cause Asher to look blurry. I don't want to cry. A migraine hits me because of my sobbing makes it difficult to think.

"How?" I rasp. Emotion chokes me, the grip so fierce and painful; I cough to release the tension on my esophagus. "Why?" Another question that lingers in the air. It's heavy, dripping with an agony so profuse I feel my heart leaping from my chest. Slamming against my ribs like a wild animal, causing a real ache.

"He was the one who helped your father update his will. He knew about the condition that you needed to be married to inherit the estate. Michael was the one

who suggested it to your father," Asher tells me with no emotion behind his words. It's as if he's shut himself off.

"And he's been using me all this time. He lied to me, making me trust him, and he's the one I've needed to kill all this time." My body is wrapped in anger. My heart, however, is wrapped in love. In Asher's love. "Why didn't you tell me on the plane, or . . . I don't know. Why didn't you come back sooner?"

He's silent for so long I'm certain he won't answer me. Then he lifts those mocha orbs to me, and the emotion swimming in them drags me into their depths. He's been my home ever since I was a little girl, and it's where I feel safe. And now, I want nothing more than to be in his arms.

"I needed time, baby. You were so broken, and there was nothing I could do but wait until you were ready. Until I was ready. There were so many moments I wanted to step out of the shadows and into your life. Tell you why I was here. But I knew you didn't remember me. You couldn't have."

"I guess you're right. My mind was broken." My agreement hurts because as much as I love Asher now,

I know it's only because I loved him then. Nothing could've prepared me for the onslaught of the emotions that came spiraling back, but he is the one who made it okay. He healed me.

"Michael planned on me never returning and you falling in love with him," Asher says then, dragging me from my morbid thoughts.

"But he knows I cared for him. I mean, he trained me. Why didn't he push for the marriage earlier?" The blaze of jealousy in Asher's eyes tells me this is not an easy subject for him. I don't blame him, but we need everything out in the open before we can ever make this work.

"He wanted your father out of the way. My dad was planning to have you and Michael take over the Calloway Organization, drugs and weapons at his disposal. He would've been king."

"How do you know?" I ask, wrapping my arms around myself. I'm not sure why I don't feel at ease or safe, but when Asher looks at me again, a cold shiver causes goosebumps to rise on my skin.

"I have ways and means, Eliana. For the years I've

been away, I haven't been far from you. Each moment you thought you were alone, I was there, watching, waiting. I kept tabs on you all your life because I loved you. I wasn't going to let some asshole walk in and take what's mine." A small smile plays on the corner of his mouth, and those dimples that make my stomach flip flop appear and deepen as he regards me.

"So, you're a stalker?" I quip, offering a sweet yet innocent smile.

His arms circle me, pulling me onto his lap. Once I'm straddling him, I twine my hands around his neck, holding on for dear life.

"Baby girl, I'd fucking stalk you to the ends of the earth. You're mine. Always will be." His words instill the safety I lacked only moments ago.

"I remember you telling me that," I say. Leaning in, I plant a soft kiss on his check. The scruff on his jaw tickles me, and I revel in the roughness of his body and the gentleness of his words.

"It seems those days are coming back to you full force," he says softly, his lips against my cheek. The movement so sweet, romantic, nothing like the passion

that he's offered me before. His hands are strong and firm on my hips, holding me to him. "What else do you recall in that pretty little head?"

"For some reason, I remember how we did homework together, listened to music on the front lawn of the mansion." My words grant me a smile. "I remember the first day you kissed me," I tell him, meeting his gaze.

"Do you remember the day I took you to the forest behind the Calloway mansion?" he questions, a sinful grin curling his lips, dark orbs twinkling with mischief.

"I do." I can feel the blush on my cheeks. My face is warm with embarrassment. "It was the first time you made me come," I tell him easily, meeting his handsome face.

"Tell me, Eliana. I want to know how I did it. Remind me," he says in a tone that's almost pained. As if he's once again holding onto restraint that causes his body to vibrate. "Close your eyes, doll face. Tell me exactly what you remember."

"You laced your fingers through mine, and we walked in between the trees, the thick trunks hiding us from view," I recall it so vividly it's as if I'm right

there in the moment. "It was so quiet all I heard were our footsteps on the fallen leaves. I was wearing a blue dress, and I kept telling you it's cold."

I can't help smiling at that because I'd never felt more alive, yet I couldn't stop shivering. It was coming up to winter, and I remember forgetting my sweater on the bed.

"When we got deeper into the forest, you pressed me against the trunk. Your body felt like granite, hard and toned," I continue, my hips now rolling against his hardness, which is right at my core.

"Do you feel the hard and toned part of me now?" I can hear the smile in his voice as he asks me the question.

"I've always felt it, ached for it."

"When you fucked the man who killed your father, did you wish it was me?" His voice laced with jealousy. It's a dangerous emotion that twirls itself around a desire for someone.

My eyes snap open, and I regard him with a narrowed stare. "Even when I didn't know who you were, I knew my heart was never with Michael. It was you. I just couldn't remember." The raw honesty I now

confess with cements my emotions. "I've loved you all my life."

"So, I shouldn't be jealous of you kissing Darick?" he teases, gripping my hips as I sit astride him. As soon as he says it though, the memory comes flooding back. The day Darick kissed me under the apple tree in our garden.

After remembering the night of my birthday, the day Meredith was killed, it's as if the floodgates have opened and I'm a fountain of memories. The day in question, I remember Darick asking me if he'd ever stand a chance against his brother. As close as the three of us were, it was always Asher. It's as if when I saw him, my heart knew. The force he entered my life with was something I never felt again.

"That day was purely him wanting to know if he had a chance," I confess. "But I told him there was never a choice. We, the three of us, there was something special between us, that much was clear." I meet Asher's gaze. He's not jealous; I can tell by the look in his eyes. "We were different, but I loved you. My heart was always going to be yours."

The moment is broken when the door flies open, and the man in question is standing on the threshold of the bedroom.

"We need to get back home. Michael has pushed the domino, and soon they're all going to fall." His cryptic words send my heart leaping into my throat. Asher rises, his hands cupping my ass. I'm attached to him like a goddamn spider monkey, but he doesn't let go until he's turned around and sets me on the bed.

"Get dressed," he orders me before heading to the doorway. "Is the jet fueled?" his question directed at Darick who nods in response.

"Ready and waiting," his brother tells him and leaves us in the bedroom.

One small glance from Asher tells me the shit is about to go down. I'm not sure why I'm nervous, but I am. Seeing Michael, knowing he killed my father, will be the ultimate test. I've wanted revenge for such a long time, but now that it's finally here, I doubt myself. *Can I kill someone I've known for half my life? Someone I slept with, allowed inside my body?*

My phone drags me from my thoughts, and when

I glance at the number, a tingle of fear trickles through me. *Uknown.*

"What do you want?" I gritted through clenched teeth.

He's silent for a moment before speaking. "Is that any way to speak to me?" There's a bite of anger in his voice, but I don't care anymore. I no longer want what he offers me. "You do realize I hold the fate of your life in my hands, Poppet," he continues, and I can hear the smirk in his tone.

"I'll kill you. I swear on my life. I'll make you pay for what you did."

"Poppet, you've always been so beautiful when you were stronger." The tone of his voice changes, but my breath catches in my throat when I realize who it is. I thought it was Asher fucking with my head, but it's not him. It's someone I least expected.

"It's you," I murmur as shock grips me tight in its grasp. "I'll tell him the truth," I vow before I hang up, not giving him a chance to respond and race from the room.

The plane touches down with a jolt, causing me to snap my eyes open and find two sets of matching brown eyes. Darick and Asher are watching me so intently it steals my breath.

"You're quite something, darling," Darick says as a smirk tugs at the corner of his mouth. Asher turns to his brother, pinning him with a glare that causes me to shiver.

"Thank you, Darick." My response earns me a look from the man I love. "What?"

"Don't worry. My brother is just worried that if you ever experienced my dick, you'd leave him for me," Darick responds, slapping Asher on the shoulder as he rises and heads for the opened door.

"Asshole," Asher quips as he gets up and pulls me into his arms.

We disembark the plane and find the cars waiting for us. Darick takes his, and I slip into the passenger seat beside Asher. The drive home is quiet, but when we take a turn to the place I haven't stepped foot in for almost

five years, I gasp.

"Why are we going to the Calloway estate?"

"We need time to regroup before you see Michael and Sean. And we need to rest. It's late." Asher's no-nonsense tone tells me not to argue, so I exit the car, and we head inside. Memories flicker through my mind — my father, my sister, and even my mother.

We make our way to the west side of the house where the guest rooms are. I cannot be near my old bedroom right now. With all I've learned, my heart aches.

"I'm heading into the shower," Asher tells me, and I nod. Needing a moment to breathe, I sit on the bed, my mind still reeling with what happened in this house. I listen to the water of the shower. From where I'm sitting, I can see Asher's body, dripping wet, suds of lather over his tanned, toned flesh.

I pull out my blade, the one that's kept me safe all these years, and toy with it. I'm lost in my own head when the water is turned off, and moments later, a half-naked Asher walks into the space. A towel wrapped around slim hips taunts me as the water drips down his chiseled torso. The planes of his body are toned to

perfection.

"Vixen," he smirks, as he moves toward me. "What's running around in that pretty little head?"

"Everything is surreal. Make it stop. Just . . ." I glance up into his shimmering eyes. He offers me a hand, which I accept. "I want the pain to stop for a moment."

His hands move down to my ass, gripping it painfully, then he lifts me against him. Asher walks us toward the wall beside the window, leaning in to press a kiss on my neck. His lips cause a tingle to shoot through me. "Like perhaps, this," he whispers, rolling his hips as he presses me against the dressing table. His erection tents the towel, and I have to bite my lip to stifle my moan.

"Just like that," I tell him, but his fingers are already teasing the thin straps of my tank top. I need it. My coping mechanism, sex, fucking, whatever you want to call it.

He doesn't respond. Instead, he pulls me up to stand, his hands landing on my hips, spinning me around. One large hand presses on my back, forcing me to bend over. He tugs my tights down my legs to find the thong I'm

wearing.

"You're a naughty girl, Eliana," he growls. "Do you like being wet for me?" He reaches for the knife in my hand, and I relinquish it to him. "Open your fucking legs." His voice is stern, commanding, and I obey. The cool steel trails its way from my shoulder blades, over the thin material of my top, and then he grips the string of my thong and slices it away.

"Asher," I whimper when I feel the cool handle of the knife at my core. The heat of my body and the chilly metal cause me to gasp in response. My knees are wobbly, and my whole body is alight as if he's struck a match and dropped it on dry timber, lighting it up causing an inferno.

"Wet and needy," he coos in my ear then. His hand puts pressure on the knife, and the handle slips into my pussy. "Is your cunt pulsing around the handle, vixen?" The pleasure spirals through me, and I can't speak. It's wrong, dangerous, but the fear does something to me. It causes my nipples to harden and my core to drip.

"Please, Asher." My whimper is nothing more than a mewl.

"Beg me, baby. Plead for me to use you." He knows what I like, what I need to get off. When I'm turned on like this, nothing can satiate me like a rough and hard fuck. He pulls out and pushes back in, fucking me with the handle.

I'm clawing at the wood, trying to ground myself, but I can't find purchase on the surface. My knees wobble, and my eyes roll back as he continues to fuck me. I feel his thumb on my puckered entrance as he circles it gently, his other hand violating me in the best way possible.

"Come, Eliana. Come all over the knife." His words echo somewhere in my brain. His taunts, his movements send me into the darkness, and I'm standing on the precipice, ready to leap. When his thumb pushes past the ring of muscle without lubricant, my body locks as the pain and pleasure sear through me like a wildfire. I cry out his name, my nails raking on the slippery counter, and I'm beyond euphoria.

He pulls the knife from my body, spins me around, and stares at me for a moment before he smirks and lifts me onto the wooden top. "Open your mouth," he

orders, and I do. The handle, drenched in my juices, is in my mouth, muffling my moans as his cock slides into me. My legs wrap around his waist as he pulls out slow and torturous, then slams into me, knocking the breath from my lungs. I'm holding on for dear life as his body owns mine.

He grips me with one hand and with the other, pulls the blade from my mouth, trailing the sharp point over my cleavage. He presses it into my flesh as his cock thrusts into me, plunging deeper and deeper. A sting on the curve of my breast causes me to snap my gaze down. The tiny pinprick is seeping blood, and his mouth is on me. He feasts on my blood while he drives his cock into me.

My toes curl, my nails clawing down his back as my body succumbs to another orgasm that shatters through me, and a cry is lodged in my throat. Pleasure chokes me as I drench us both in my juices. The room spins, and I have to hold onto him to keep from falling because it feels as if my world is off kilter.

"I'll always give you what you need," he says with confidence. And he's right.

Quickly, he lifts me and walks us both to the bed, curling on the mattress behind me, he tugs me into his hold until sleep steals me.

"You ready for this, vixen? If you don't want to see him, you don't have to," he tells me with honesty shining in his eyes.

"I need this, Asher. As long as you're there, I can do it," I respond. Michael sent me a message asking me to meet him at the warehouse on the pier as soon as we landed. I'm scared of what I'm capable of, but something deep inside reminds me I've been training for this most of my life. The only problem is that Michael was the one training me.

We silently made our way to the warehouse. Asher and Darick move like hunters in the darkness. The moon is hiding behind the cloud bank, and the only light comes from the rooftop of the building before us. My anxiety is skyrocketing with each step we take. The knife in my hand is gripped so tight the blood flow in my fingers is non-existent.

"Eliana, you'll fall behind me. Darick, you're behind her. If he comes from the front or back, I want us to take him." Asher's words are hushed, his eyes on his brother as he speaks. "He doesn't touch her." His serious tone vibrates through me.

I've never been scared in a fight, never allowed myself to let fear take hold of me. But each time I've been on the job, Michael has been the one beside me. He knows my moves, everything I can do. He taught me, and that makes him a danger to me. And Asher knows this.

Darick steps up behind me, the heat of his body warming my back makes me breathe easier. "Time to play, kitten," he murmurs in my ear as we step into the warehouse. Water dripping sounds from within the cavernous space. Our feet crunching on the dirty cement floor seems to ring in my ears.

"I thought you'd come alone, baby girl." Michael's voice comes from the darkness. My gaze shoots up to the balcony on the far end of the room to find him.

"I thought you were a good man. It seems we both miscalculated the other," I call out to him. My voice

echoes around us. "Why don't you come down here and we can talk," I say. Seeing him now, knowing he killed my father, only cements the fact that I have to make him pay. And when he does, it's going to be by my hand.

"Why don't you ask your little friends to wait outside? This is between you and me, is it not?" he quips back. The satisfaction in his voice makes me sick. The anger I'd harbored all these years for my father's murderer races through me now, and all I feel is rage.

"Perhaps," I tell him. Asher looks at me, worry written all over his face. He's exhausted, so am I, but I need him to trust me. "I'll be okay. I need to do this alone."

He's warring with himself, with me, silently, but I see it in his expression. He doesn't want to leave me alone with Michael. But I implore him with my gaze to trust me. He nods once, then turns, leaning in his mouth in at my ear. "If he so much as lays a hand on you, I'll kill him."

The threat is clear. I nod. Then I'm alone in the dark with a killer.

The sound of his shoes on the metal staircase

resounds with an ominous clatter. I know why he chose this place. The noises as they whirl together in a chorus is enough to make anyone fearful lose their mind.

Drip. Clank. Drip. Clank.

He taught me this. How to make your opponent weak by using your surroundings. The thing he didn't bank on was me stealing myself to it. His game no longer holds power over me.

"You know, all those nights I was buried deep inside you, I thought you'd love me one day," he says as he strolls closer to me one controlled, calculated step at a time.

I'm in fighting stance, my legs shoulder-width apart, knees locked, the knife in my hand ready to slice into him. I don't respond; I can't because yes, at one point I thought perhaps I did love him, but I know better.

"The day I took your virginity was my favorite. You cried when I tore into you. The way you loved it rough, needed it all the time. It was—"

"Are we going to stand here all day reminiscing about how many times we fucked?" I question, interrupting his words I know are meant to throw me

off my game.

"You know this is all about sex and money. I mean, what else were you expecting?" he asks, inches from me. His dark eyes are glowing with danger as he regards me.

I could easily lift my hand and lodge the blade in his chest, but I know he's fast. He'll stop me before I make contact. I need to play this calmly. He reaches for me, gripping my hair at the nape of my neck and tugs my head back. When he leans in, I feel his hot breath on my face. My heart thumps against my ribs, painful and fast.

His other hand snakes toward my hand that holds my weapon, and he lifts it to his neck. I want to steal my fear, stop it from showing, but my hand trembles. When he presses the sharp side to his flesh, I watch in awe as it gently breaks the skin and a small trickle of blood drips from the tiny wound.

"Does it turn you on, little dove?" he murmurs, his lips turning up into a smirk as he watches my eyes follow the trail of crimson. "I know you enjoyed it. Didn't you? The thrill of the kill; the hunt made you wet and needy."

"Yes, it was the fact that I took someone's life that turned me on, not you. Don't mistake what I got from

you for anything more than a quick fuck," I bite out.

He releases my hand, leaving the knife at his throat. "Do it," he taunts. His eyes blaze with desire and hunger. Feral and animalistic. "Or perhaps you should prove to me that you can fight. Hand to hand combat. Let's see if the student can take down the teacher." He steps back, and my hand falls to my side.

"Tell me why you killed my father?" I ask. Stalking in a circle around him, we move in sync, the same way we always did in training. He faces me, and we're now both in combat stance. I slip the blade into the holster on my thigh and hold up both hands.

His movement is like a predator, fast and deadly as his fist slams into my face sending me reeling backward. Not wasting time, he swipes his leg at my ankles, causing my body to hit the floor with a resounding thud.

"I thought you'd have figured it out," he says. Suddenly, he's in my face, his hand slamming hard into my stomach, causing me to double over and curl into a ball. My gasps are loud and quick. I try to pull in air the way he taught me and right myself.

The pain is enough to have anyone not getting

up easily, but I've been trained. His foot knocks me completely breathless. I watch him step back through blurry eyes.

"I wanted to take over the Calloway fortune, and you could've been my queen. Do you realize what you've lost?" he hisses angrily. I know I've not lost anything because if inheriting my father's organization means having Michael in my life, I'd rather walk away from it. This life is something I was born into, and as much as I love the rush, the danger, if I can have a normal life, I'll take it.

His feet stalk around me, and I watch like he used to tell me to do. When we trained, he never hurt me. It was always fake punches and kicks, but this is more than I've ever experienced, the pain shooting through every part of me. The door flies open, and Asher is there. His gaze falling on me, but before he can come closer, Michael turns and faces him.

"Unless you want her to die a gruesome death, I suggest you step back. This is between her and me," he informs Asher.

"It's fine. I'm fine," I wheeze.

While his attention is on Asher, I manage to push myself onto my hands and knees. The agony of his attack causes me to cough and splutter as I right myself. My gaze lifts to the dark eyes of the man I love, and I give him a nod.

Once my breathing is back to normal, I move swiftly. Spinning on my one heel, I allow my other leg to fly through the air in a roundhouse kick, making contact with Michael's face. The blood that drips from his mouth looks obscene when he smiles — pearly white teeth drenched in the cherry red.

"Good girl. You've finally got that right," he says.

I don't waste time. My hand flies out in an uppercut punch, and his nose cracks from the contact. His fist thuds into my face, sending me spinning to the ground. Before I have time move, he's on me with his thick muscled thighs on either side of my hips. Both his calloused hands are around my throat, tightening by the second.

I claw at his arms, but nothing stops him. The lightheaded feeling of having my breath cut off takes over, and my eyes roll back. Asher is closing in, but I

want to do this. I need to do this. I have to find a way to get him off me.

"Eliana!" The voice sounds from Asher as if it's miles away.

"I bet your little cunt is wet right now. You always loved breath play," he coos in my ear. The words send a violent surge through me, and my hand grips the handle of the knife, which I bring up swiftly, shoving it into the side of his throat. Blood spurts from the hole as I twist it inside him. His eyes are wide with shock. "You've learned well, baby girl," Michael gurgles with his lips on my flesh.

When I pull out the blade, I stab him in the ribs. I continue, pulling it out and forcing it back until his body goes limp above me. I can't move; the shock of what I've just done paralyzes me for a moment.

The warmth of blood drenching me, his final words, and the relief I feel at finally getting my revenge all crash through me, and I find myself crying.

ASHER

Her body shudders as I rip the asshole off her. She's soaked in blood; her skin red, her clothes a dark Merlot color, while her white hair has streaks of the filthy scum's blood through it.

"Baby." I pull her against me, my arms wrapping around her.

She's crying silently into my neck while Darick drags the body away from her. He doesn't say anything, leaving me to console her from the world.

"I did it," she mumbles. Her words are muffled by my shirt, the sound of her voice raspy with emotion. I've never killed for revenge. It's always been a job, but I know the two differ vastly. It's a choice you make, to take a life because of anger, because of the need to satiate your hunger for vengeance.

"Let's go get you cleaned up," I tell her, planting a

kiss on the top of her head.

Watching her fight him was the most challenging thing I've ever done besides walking away from her all those years ago. The moment I saw her go down, I wanted to save her, but I knew deep down she had to do this on her own. She's strong. More so than I ever imagined, and seeing her take down Michael was incredible.

Lifting her, I stalk out toward the Jeep. Darick opens the door as we near him. He offers a nod, which tells me he took care of the body. Once I've got Eliana settled and the door is closed, I meet his inquiring stare.

"I don't think we'll go see dad tonight. She's too wrung out, and I'm tired," I tell him, casting a quick glance in the car at Eliana. Her eyes are fluttering, and I know she's about to pass out.

"Let's go to the Calloway mansion, get some rest, and tomorrow we'll have to see Sean," Darick says. He's right, it will be easier being there than going near our father right now.

I nod, turning toward the Jeep and slip into the driver's seat, while Darick joins me in the passenger side with Eliana curled in the back. Silence surrounds us as I

drive down familiar streets. It's coming to a head, and I don't know how we'll all find our closure, but one thing I know for sure is that Sean Briggs will die whether it's by her hand or mine.

All these years I planned and plotted. I wanted to come back and tell her everything, but when I arrived at her father's funeral and saw her with Michael, something inside me snapped. I wanted to rage through the crowd and push him into the six-foot-deep hole and bury him along with her father. But I knew that she wouldn't remember me. And for her to have closure, she needed to face her past with my father.

I'm a believer in revenge, in facing your demons, and after what happened to her, I know she needs to talk to Sean, get all that anger off her chest, and lay her sister's memory to rest.

When I open my eyes, Eliana is sitting in the window seat of the bedroom.

"We need to talk, Asher. I know who the caller is," she says as if she can feel my gaze on her. We've always

had a connection like this, ingrained in each other's being.

"Are you talking to me, or yourself, baby girl?" I question. Pushing off the bed, I pad over to her. She turns to me then, her eyes peering up at me.

"It's your father," she tells me.

"What?" My throat burns as I furrow my brows in confusion. Darick said it was Michael. Actually . . . He didn't say that. He told me the video came from the Briggs mansion, and we both assumed it was him.

"I recognized him when he called the last time. It's Sean. It was him all along."

I'm still confused. Something isn't adding up. The door to her bedroom flies open, and I turn to find Darick in his black briefs with disheveled hair.

"Dillon called," he informs us, closing the distance between us. His eyes meet mine. "You killed Mr. O'Connell. Didn't you?"

The job I did where I fucked a young wife comes back to me instantaneously. I nod.

"Michael O'Connell and the man you killed were brothers. Michael had a penchant for young women just

like his brother, and just like our father."

"So, Michael wanted revenge on Asher for killing his brother. What does this have to do with me?" Eliana questions. She rises, her bare feet padding toward the closet as she grabs a pair of sweatpants and sweater.

"Meredith and Michael were together, but . . ." Darick's gaze flits between us, and something in my gut tells me a bomb is about to drop and explode all over our fucking lives.

"But what, Darick?" I prompt my brother because this is getting fucking ridiculous.

"Your sister was having an affair with my father." And there it is — the grenade of all fucking grenades. I feel sick to think my father was with a girl who is more than half his age.

"How . . ." Eliana's voice cracks. "How do you know?"

"The video that was sent," Darick tells us. "There's a lot more where that one came from." A shudder races through Eliana's body, and the revulsion is clear on her face.

"We need to end this. Now."

She's right. I nod. So does Darick.

We enter the mansion without anyone noticing. There aren't any maids or security staff, which I find rather unsettling. Eliana is behind me as we make our way to the office that holds so many secrets. When I push the door open, my father sits back with a smile on his face.

"I was wondering how long it would take you to come to me."

Eliana saunters by me, closing the distance between my father and her. She's in his face, and I watch in awe as her tiny fist makes contact with his cheek. Rage explodes through him, and he grips her neck, shoving her backward until she's slamming into the glass window of his patio door.

I lift my gun, aiming it at his chest.

"Can you kill your old man, Asher?"

"How about you tell us the truth, *old man*," I bite back. Darick is helping Eliana up. She wanted to know what happened; that's the only reason I'm not watching his blood drain from a bullet hole.

His cold eyes fall on Eliana. "Your sister was decadent. Her sweet cunt was so delicious each time I tasted it," he says in a tone that causes her to retch. "You were meant to be next, Eliana. I was so close to claiming both your bodies. Did you know your sister was pregnant when you brutally killed her?" he asks, his tone calm, calculated, and ominous.

I watch my girl's eyes fill with unshed tears. Guilt must be eating at her. But this isn't her fault. It's the man in front of her.

"You're a sick bastard," she hisses, lifting the knife from her belt.

"At least I own up to it. My sons will never be able to do what I did because they're weak. If you hadn't lost your fucking mind, I would've been ruling the Calloway fortune right now. But no, my sons had to interfere."

"What was your plan? To marry me off to Michael?"

"Oh no, my dear. He was collateral damage. You would've married me. Bore my children, like your sister was meant to. When you murdered her, I got rid of my sons in order to keep you from them. Keep your mind free of what happened, and when you turned twenty-

five, I would've taken you. Put a baby inside you."

I watch as the man I grew up with confesses. And with each word, I feel even sicker than I did before.

"I would never have let you do that," Eliana retorts, anger dripping from her words.

"I don't care what you would've let me do. There's one thing you don't realize, Poppet. I don't ask, I take." Suddenly, my father pulls his gun, and I watch in slow motion as the barrel points at Eliana. I shout out, racing to her, but the shot rings through the room. Except it's not Eliana that goes down, it's Darick.

I'm on my brother as Eliana kicks the gun from Sean's hand. Darick shudders as I pull him up.

"I'm fine. I've been waiting for this moment all my life." He glances at the blood spilling from the gunshot wound. None of the staff would be around this wing of the house, so I know my brother is headed to find one. "Just look after her," he tells me, and I realize it's just a flesh wound.

For the first time in my life, I feel relief.

Darick smirks, "Go one, Asher, get the girl."

I have no idea what my brother means, but I nod and

turn on my father. He's fighting Eliana, her body moving in ways I've never seen before. She swivels, ducks from the blows he's trying to land, and when he kicks her feet from under her, she leaps back up in seconds.

He can't get to her, and that's when I lunge for him. The man before me shivers as I pin him down. Eliana's eyes glow with excitement. She's was born for this. Her hand slowly slices through the tanned flesh, and she smirks.

"You see, revenge is something not everyone can master." Her words drip venom. A viper that's finally caught its prey. I watch in awe as her hand presses the now blood-covered blade to his esophagus, and I hear the crack of bone. "But I will forever revel in the fact that you got what you deserve," she hisses in his face. The crimson liquid that spurts over her only makes her laugh.

"Y-your f-father would b-be p-pr-proud." His last and final words uttered, and I know they must sting. She loved Mr. Calloway, and the fact that she's finally taken his murderer down will be her retribution. She smiles as her hand rears back and her fist meets his nose. Another

loud crunch and the life drains from his body.

I realized after she killed Michael she would never be sated until my father was dead. Neither would I. But as I look at his body, I know justice has been served. Yes, there were days, months, years I wanted to return and kill him myself, but it wasn't for me to do. I wanted her to do it so she could have the closure she needed.

"I'm going to grab Dillon to sort this out," Darick says, his hand still holding the wound. "Eliana, you're perfect." He smirks, "I'll be back, brother." He offers me a wink, and I know he's happy, the emotion dancing in his gaze.

Once we're along, Ellie glances at me, a small smile of relief on her face.

My father took everything from her, but she's now reclaimed it. Everything will be hers. Even me. Like I've always been. There was never a day that went by that she didn't own me. Her smile would grant me the calm I needed each time I walked into a home, building, or warehouse to murder. And every time I walked out, it was the memory of her that seemed to make me feel like once all this was over, I could be a better man.

"I'm done," she murmurs. Turning to me, I notice her body caked in the blood of a Briggs. Her gaze drops to her tank top and tight-fitting black combat pants. "Do I look pretty?" She smiles up at me, trailing the knife along the material of her tank top. Her flesh, cherry red, shimmers in the light of the moon.

"You look good enough to fuck," I tell her. Stepping closer, I grip the knife and press it to her body. The material falls away from the sharpness of the silver, and she's only wearing a tiny jet-colored bra that cups her tits.

"Perhaps you should take advantage," she purrs like a kitten in my ear, and my cock agrees that we should indeed take advantage.

"You want to fuck over a dead body?" I ask incredulously.

"Isn't your cock hard from watching me?" she taunts, her hand traveling down to my slacks, finding my rigid erection pressing against her hand. "I thought so," she tells me.

"Suck my dick with your blood-covered lips," I order, watching her drop to her knees before me. A

pool of thick, metallic crimson soaks her pants, but she doesn't even flinch. The woman is a goddess, a fucking dangerous vixen. She pulls my dick from my pants, not lowering it, but through the open zipper, and wraps her plump lips covered in our enemy's blood around the crown.

A pleasured hiss leaves my lips. "Fuck, yes, doll face," I tell her, my voice husky, filled with hunger. She continues sliding her hot mouth down the shaft until I hit the base of her throat. The scene before me is so fucked up, but I can't stop myself. I need this. I need her.

She gurgles, choking on me as she takes me deeper than ever before, and my knees just about give out. I need to hold onto something or I'll fall to the ground. I'm about to grip her hair when she lets up and rises to her full height.

"Fuck me, Asher. Right here and now." My hands are on her ass. Lifting her, I walk us toward the wall and fumble with her pants until she's naked from the waist down. My cock slides along her slit, feeling the slick wetness of her arousal, and I groan once more.

Rolling my hips, I slide into her easily. She's

drenched. Her juices drip down my cock. "Look at him on the floor," I tell her as I pump into her body. "You did it. You're strong and beautiful. And now you're mine." Her nails claw my shoulders and back as I fuck her relentlessly. Her gaze is pinned behind me on the lifeless form of my father. His blood is soaking us both as if we're being baptized in the retribution Eliana has taken for what he's done.

"Fuck," her voice is hoarse as she cries out profanities. "Fuck, yes," she moans in my ear. My mouth finds purchase on her shoulder, the metallic taste in my mouth as I bite down on her flesh. Wanting to taste her and only her. "Asher!" she screams as I thrust deep, all the way into her tight little cunt, and my teeth the break skin as I suck the delicious sweetness of her lifeforce. Like a vampire feeding, it only heightens my need, my desire, my hunger for her.

"Come on my dick, my little doll," I growl as I feel my balls drawing up. Tightening. Her body pulses around me. Milking me. And I give it to her freely.

"Yes!" she whimpers, her mewls louder, feral, and her body finds release in the dark where we play with

our demons.

EPILOGUE

ELIANA

Five months later

There's been a lot of talk about what happened to Mr. Briggs. And even though there's been speculation that one of his enemies took his life, the secret that we hold will die with the four of us. Darick stalks into the office, the look on his face severe. I don't greet him. Instead, I stare as he settles himself opposite me.

"I'm leaving. There are things I need to do. I've always been here waiting for the moment I can walk away, and it's come now that this is all sorted out."

My ears ring with the words he's just rattled off. "What?"

He rises, placing an envelope on the desk. My name scrawled in black ink on the front.

"Read that." Two words and he's out the door. Frowning at my soon-to-be brother-in-law, I shake my head and rip open the manila envelope. A letter folded in four sits between my trembling fingers. As soon as I open it, I recognize the writing immediately.

My gaze devours the words, those same words explaining what Meredith had planned. She wanted to get pregnant with Sean's child and get rid of me. But he was the one who didn't want the plan to come to fruition. He loved me. Crumpling the page, I trash it, not believing a man like that could love anything but himself.

There have been whispers about Meredith being alive within the client list of Sean's organization, but even though Darick has been scouring for her, nothing's come up just yet. I thought I'd killed her, and with the words left in this letter, it confirms my sister is dead.

She'd held on to so much misery just to get back at me for the jealousy she harbored for me as we grew up. Learning that she was sleeping with a man who was old

enough to be our father, that she planned on one day having his children was the strangest, the sickest thing I'd ever heard of.

Asher and I have decided to shut down both our father's organizations. It's time to move on from the darkness and step into a life with our family. The danger is behind us, and I'm thankful he's chosen our children and me over the shit his father did.

Darick is moving to London, and I'm happy he has the freedom to no longer kill for a man who was a criminal. I don't blame him for wanting to leave. If I didn't have the Calloway mansion to care for, to look after, I'd have asked Asher if we could leave. But as the weeks wear on, it makes being here easier, and knowing that in these rooms we'll soon have children running riot.

My stomach pulses as our twins kick at my body. They're due soon enough, and I can't wait to become a mother. Picking up the phone, I hit dial on the number, knowing it's late, but Asher is on his way home from a job, and I feel lonely for the first time in a long while.

Three rings and the familiar English accent comes

from the other end of the line.

"Hello, darling," Dillon greets me.

"How are you?" I settle back in Asher's leather chair. Closing my eyes, I picture the first day in Dillon's office when he licked my pussy and made me come all over his tongue.

"Better hearing your delicious voice, sweetheart." I can hear the smile on his face, and I can't stop the one that curls on mine. "When are the babies due?"

"Soon. I have another four months to go, and that will fly by," I tell him, listening to him hum over the line, and I know he's probably working.

"I can't wait to be an uncle," he tells me earnestly. And he will be. He may not be blood, but he is as close to us as Darick is. "Tell those two that Uncle Dillon says they better behave because when I get there, we'll have a week of debauchery. And if you're a good girl, I might even give you a little taste of my tongue again," he rasps down the line, and my hand falls to my breasts which are heavy due to my hormones that tug me in every direction.

"Tell me," I beg, needing more. My hormones have

been all over the place since I've been pregnant, and I am so turned on, I need an orgasm. But the other reason I'm doing this is that I know Asher will be home soon, and I'm hoping he catches me.

"I'll lie you down on the bed. While your man plunges his beautiful cock in your mouth, I'll lick and finger your sweet hole until you're crying out." His voice is merely a whisper, but I hear every word.

"Are you having fun, vixen?" Asher grunts from the doorway and I jolt up.

Caught red-handed, I blush. "Perhaps," I tell him, still speaking into the phone.

"Why don't you and Dillon continue? I'll devour that pretty little cunt of yours." And that's how my two men are. One on the other side of the world, and my future husband kneeling between my thighs.

ACKNOWLEDGMENTS

Allyson, you have been an angel working with me through this intense journey. Thank you for everything, I can't tell you how much I appreciate you. Thank you for putting up with my every changing eye color! ;)

Thank you to my BETA's—Alicia, Allyson, Cat—you ladies are amazing. I don't know how I could do this without you!

Candy, my editor, I don't know what I'd do without you. You're stuck with me, woman!

A huge thanks to my my Angels street team—Tre, Sheena, Sarah, Lisa, Caroline, TJ, Hayfaah, Joy, Cinders, Kathy, Sara, Tanya—thank you for pimping my work EVERYWHERE. You ladies rock!!

My reader group, The Darklings, as always, you're the only place I know I'll find like-minded ladies and a handful of gents who will have a laugh without drama.

The group has grown so much and I'm excited for the future! Thank you for being there.

To all my author colleagues, thank you for always sharing, commenting, and supporting me. I appreciate every one of you. Having a support system is important and you ladies provide that and so much more.

Readers and bloggers, from the bottom of my little black heart, THANK YOU. All you do for us authors is incredible. Reading and reviewing is demanding on your own time and you do it with a smile. Thank you so, so much. You are valued and appreciated for taking time out to show us so much love.

If you enjoyed this story, please consider leaving a review. I'd love you forever. (Even though I already do!)

ABOUT DANI

Dani is a USA Today Bestselling Author of dark and deviant romance with a seductive edge.

Originally from Cape Town, South Africa, she now lives in the UK with her better half who does all the cooking while she writes all the words.

When she's not writing, she can be found binge-watching the latest TV series, or working on graphic design either for herself, or other indie authors. She enjoys reading books about handsome villains and feisty heroines, mostly dark, always seductive, and sometimes depraved.

She has a healthy addiction to tattoos, coffee, and ice cream.

www.danirene.com

info@danirene.com

FIND DANI ONLINE

Do you follow me?

If not, head over to any of the below links,

I love to hear from my readers!

Amazon - http://bit.ly/DaniAmazon

BookBub - http://bit.ly/DaniBookBub

Facebook - http://bit.ly/DaniFBPage

Facebook Group - Dani's Deviants

Goodreads - http://bit.ly/DaniGoodreads

Twitter - @danireneauthor

Pinterest - @danireneauthor

Instagram - @danireneauthor

Spotify - http://bit.ly/DaniSpotify

OTHER BOOKS

Stand Alones

Choosing the Hart

Love Beyond Words

Cuffed

Fragile Innocence

Perfectly Flawed

Black Light: Obsessed

Among Ash and Ember

Within Me (Limited Time)

Cursed in Love (collaboration with Cora Kenborn)

Beautifully Brutal (Soldati di Sangue)

How the Mind Breaks

The Devil's Plaything

While She Sleeps (Dirty Heroes Collection)

It's Never Easy (Lady Boss Press)

Only One Night (Lady Boss Press)

Deviant (Black Mountain Academy)

TABOO NOVELLAS

Sunshine and the Stalker (collab. with K Webster)

His Temptation

Austin's Christmas Shortcake

Crime and Punishment (Newsletter Exclusive)

Tempting Grayson

GILDED SOVEREIGN SERIES

Cruel War (Book #1)

Volatile Love (Book #2)

SINS OF SEVEN SERIES

Kneel (Book #1)

Obey (Book #2)

Indulge (Book #3)

Ruthless (Book #4)

Bound (Book #5)

Envy (Book #6)

Vice (Book #7)

THE TAKEN SERIES

Stolen

Severed

FOUR FATHERS SERIES

Kingston

Four Sons Series

Brock

Carina Press Novellas

Pierced Ink

Madd Ink

Broken Series

Broken by Desire

Shattered by Love

The Backstage Series

Callum

Liam

Ryan

Forbidden Series

From the Ashes - A Prequel

Crave (Book #1)

Covet (Book #2)

Printed by Amazon Italia Logistica S.r.l.
Torrazza Piemonte (TO), Italy

38486557R00198